Secret of the Snail

by

Janet Ollerenshaw

Dedication

This work is dedicated to my mother,
Chris Dunn

She is an inspiration to everyone and her stoic
support of my brothers and me is unbounded and
unconditional.
Thank you for giving me a love of words and stories
and for encouraging me to write.

Acknowledgments

My heartfelt thanks go to;

All those who have encouraged me to have the
confidence to write;

My children whose acceptance of their slightly
'crazy' mother has allowed me to demonstrate my
craziness in writing;
with special thanks to Megan for her proof-reading
expertise,

My brothers who made me stronger than I believed
I could be;

And in particular, Mark, without whose constant
encouragement, love, support and unfailing
enthusiasm, this work and its predecessors may
never have materialised.

To Darin Jewell and to the many others who have
made possible the production of these books and the
realisation of a dream, I give you my everlasting
gratitude.

Thinking Out Loud

Thinking out loud; those words on the page
Scampering about; Mice out of a cage
Where are they going? What do they say?
Will they sing the same song as they sang out
today?
The pictures they sing; the emotions so strong
Without any question of rightness or wrong
Are just thoughts here on paper escaped from my
mind
And floating about just as leaves on the wind.
Patterns are forming then fading so soon
As the tides flow and ebb with the pull of the moon.
Sometimes the words whisper of secrets untold
Then shout to the mountains as mysteries unfold,
Thinking in circles, on paper, out loud,
My thoughts, my emotions, alone in a crowd.

JBO Feb. 2008

Chapter 1

Hingemont

The sleepy village almost disappeared in the onslaught of lashing rain which obscured everything more than a couple of yards in front of the slowly crawling vehicle. No lights lit the single street and the sometimes visible dim glow emanating from large houses set back from the road was similarly obliterated by the driving downpour.

Imogen peered blindly through the streaming screen, hunched forward over the wheel as she tried in vain to read an already partially obscured name board on a rickety gate. "I'm sure I'm in the right place," she murmured, though truth to tell she didn't feel very sure of anything at that precise moment.

Had it really only been three days since the summons? And why her, when she had probably been the furthest away from here? There were others like her, equally accountable, weren't there? In her head she counted her cousins; Aunty Mae had four children, Millie, three and Uncle Bo had at least five, or maybe six by now. Then of course there were her brothers; Max and Archie, so it really didn't seem reasonable that she should be the only one to take on this most recent responsibility.

Sighing deeply, she put the little car into gear, sped up the wipers to their maximum capability, at which point they waggled so frantically that it seemed they would fly right off the vehicle, and gradually proceeded further through the village. She passed, on her right, the village hall with its wildly swinging notice board which clung precariously to its gallows whilst inviting all to the forthcoming Harvest supper; not that she could read any of the information, no, that would come later, but for now it served to trigger a memory from somewhere in the depths of her mind that the house was beyond this point and that there was a gate that had to be opened, leading up a longish driveway to the large house which was her intended destination.

And suddenly, just as she was beginning to consider the merits of returning to the nearby town to find a room for the night, there it was. Surprisingly the gate stood uncomfortably open, swinging slightly in the hurricane force wind, but tenuously secured with a piece of orange twine that similarly flapped and threatened to rip itself apart. At least someone had considered the extremely inclement weather and her intended ingress. She smiled wryly and was comforted by a rustling sound from the back seat followed by a wet nose that pressed against the back of her neck. How was it that Benjy always knew when they were about to arrive somewhere? For the entire journey thus far he had remained curled up and fast asleep; not even bothering to raise his head when she was obliged to stop for fuel or at traffic lights. And now he was up on his rather short legs, shaking his rather long ears and scruffy golden hair and making it quite clear that he was ready to exit the car. It was impossible to stay irritated with Benjy for more than a second or two. His slightly lopsided comical expression and obvious delight in her company; evidenced by his wildly wagging tail and lolling pink tongue, always melted her heart and she reached behind her to fondle his wriggling body before telling him that he must wait while she assessed the situation regarding welcomes and wet feet.

She quickly abandoned the idea of using her large golfing umbrella (not acquired with any intention of ever playing golf) or indeed any umbrella, and rummaged in the capacious bag on the seat beside her. She pulled out a waterproof jacket, which by a series of improbable contortions, she managed to put on with the hood tied firmly under her chin and the zip done up as far as it would go. There was no way, in the restricted space, that she could get the matching trousers onto her legs and nor could she reach the wellington boots that were tucked behind the passenger seat and so she would just have to make a run for the house and try to stay as dry as possible. That was always assuming that the icy blast of the gale force wind didn't blow her off her feet.

The car door was almost ripped from her hand as she tentatively pulled the release handle and she found herself unceremoniously deposited in the biggest puddle imaginable. Resigning herself to an inevitable drenching, she decided that she had better close the gate too so that there was a slim chance that Benjy would not escape before she had time to check the boundaries for small, canine sized exits.

A short while later, having removed to the front porch as much of her luggage as she could carry in one go, and having returned to release Benjy from his several hours of captivity; and he having raced around the shingled driveway before relieving himself against the magnificent sundial which stood solitarily in the centre of a one-time rose bed situated in the middle of the circular entrance feature, they made a sorry and bedraggled pair as she reached up to pull the old-fashioned bell-pull which served as a doorbell.

Somewhere in the depths of the ancient house, a bell clanged faintly, followed by a resounding silence.

Imogen waited for what seemed like a long while, though in reality was not more than a few minutes. She was shivering slightly in the damp chill while Benjy sat on her feet in his usual possessive position and also waited, although more patiently than she. It was after this pause that it dawned on her that of course there was no one to open the door. No one to welcome her and no one to object to Benjy's wet feet, and it was then, having had plenty of time to consider her situation, she remembered mention of a key and a hiding place. Chiding herself for her good forgettery, she once more breached the wild weather conditions and made her tentative way around the side of the house, which, given its size, was some considerable distance, and eventually she arrived at the back porch. Once inside where it was at least dry and better sheltered, she reached up and felt along the head-height shelf and searched for the aforementioned hiding place.

It is amazing how a very long journey, a traumatic situation and exhaustion can befuddle the brain and drive away long held memories. However, as she lifted down the carved box with its secret lid which she slid open to remove the key, suddenly she was a child again and laughing delightedly as her grandfather showed her how to open the seemingly impossible puzzle box. She grinned and without further hesitation, slid the rediscovered key into the ancient lock of the heavy back door which creaked open with an impressive screech. Stepping into the once familiar red flagged kitchen, she switched on the overhead light and was unexpectedly flooded with brightness, warmth and reminiscences.

Which particular someone had prepared for her arrival, she had no idea, but she was grateful for the well stoked aga, the singing kettle on its hob and the tea tray set carefully on the kitchen table with a note which welcomed her and informed her that there was a hearty casserole in the bottom oven. In addition to this, a bed had been made up in the spare room (which she would surely remember) and the warming pan was ready for coals from the fire to be inserted and the sheets made less frosty. At the bottom of the note, scribbled in pencil and squeezed in as if in afterthought, was a phone number and an instruction to 'call me if you need anything' without any reference as to which particular 'me' the messenger might be.

Of course she remembered the spare room. How could she forget? How many nights had she spent there with her brothers and cousins? There was never much sleeping done in the big bed which had plenty of room for all five of them. There was however, much story telling; mostly ghost stories and stories designed to scare her and her younger brother, Archie, although to be truthful they were all scared witless at times. It wasn't the stories that frightened them; it was Grandfather roaring up the spiral staircase that if they weren't silent and or asleep in five minutes, he was coming up to beat them with a feather. At that time, none of them had realised that it was a physical impossibility for Grandfather to ascend the narrow stairs but the threat was enough and silence always ensued for at least another five minutes before the whispered storytelling began again and the shrieks muffled by mouthfuls of pillow corners or soft blankets.

Situated at the top of a small turret, the guest room was only accessible via the spiral stairs and so the bed, which must have been built in situ and which would have to be completely dismantled if it were ever to be removed, remained exactly as she remembered it. The rest of the spacious room had been 'modernised'; the childish curtains and wall murals replaced with a plainer and more sophisticated decor and the previous toilet table with its plastic washbowl and jug had become a small washroom with running water, the 'po' (kept under the bed) had been superseded by a proper loo and there was even an electric shower. Whichever builder had worked that particular miracle deserved a medal for ingenuity and Imogen was grateful not to have to carry a heavy jug of hot water up the three flights of stairs in order to wash herself before slipping into her fleecy onsie and between the by now well warmed sheets.

It was typical of Grandmother's thinking that despite her nod to modernisation with the ensuite; she still warmed the sheets with an old-fashioned warming pan rather than an electric blanket or even a hot water bottle. Placing the unwieldy implement on the floor Imogen glanced at her mobile phone and was astonished to discover that it was barely ten o'clock, although she was not surprised to see that there was very little signal and therefore no point in sending safe arrival messages. Deciding that it was much too early to go to sleep, she picked up the cheap novel that she had bought in a supermarket to read for a little while, but her mind would not focus on the words and the events of the last twenty four hours which had prompted her precipitate arrival here, together with her wild journey, whirled through her thoughts just as the wind whirled around the elevated turret in which she was cosily ensconced.

Eventually, lulled by the warmth of the comfortable old bed, her well satisfied stomach and the gentle snoring of Benjy who had refused to sleep in the kitchen and was now tucked under the covers with her, adding to the cosiness, her eyes began to close and the paperback fell to the floor with a soft thud. Within a very few minutes, she was sound asleep.

Chapter 2

Manston

The soft thud of papers falling to the floor immediately followed a tentative knock on his door. "Come in Amy," he growled from somewhere under the desk and he arose looking decidedly dishevelled and more than a little crumpled as she, wordlessly, placed a steaming mug of coffee carefully within his reach but not close enough to be clumsily knocked over, and left as quietly and unobtrusively as she had arrived. 'She's a gem!' he thought to himself and made a mental note to treat her more kindly than the last apology for a secretary the agency had supplied.

Percival Arthur Lancer Esquire, Solicitor and Psychologist; or more accurately Dr Lancer PhD and LL.B (hons), since the psychology doctorate had come first, on this particular morning, was not a happy man. Not only had he had a restless night but the day had not begun propitiously when his ancient car had refused to start which meant he'd had to drag out his equally antique bicycle in order to at least attempt to get to the office on time. When it was eventually extracted from beneath a pile of miscellaneous junk, the cobweb festooned bike was revealed to have two flat tyres and in desperation Arthur had returned to the house, hoping, but failing, to dodge the inevitable questioning from his aged mother, and had telephoned for an ill-affordable taxi. On top of all that, it had rained incessantly and when he finally reached the office, he was not only late but damp and uncomfortable too. The coffee was very welcome.

It was typical that these events should have happened today of all days. He had hoped to have time to peruse the wad of papers before his client arrived but now he would only have the opportunity to do little more than flick through the file, hoping to spot the most relevant points.

~

Mrs Lancer hummed tunelessly to herself as she washed the breakfast dishes. Although she was very happy to have her son living with her once more, she was more than a little dismayed at the circumstances that had led to his unexpected arrival on her doorstep little more than a month ago. She had imagined that by the age of forty-two he would be happily married with a child or two and a satisfying and lucrative career. However, despite being married to his childhood sweetheart, children had not come and he had not seemed able to settle to any particular career. There was no doubt that he was very capable and decidedly intelligent but perhaps that was the problem. He didn't suffer fools gladly and found it difficult to see the purpose in most mundane careers. Psychology had suited him well; he had even been offered a research bursary, but as usual he had turned it down because he couldn't see the point in investigating the particular area on which the University wanted him to focus. Law had fascinated him and his change of direction in qualifying as a solicitor through a Graduate Diploma in Law, followed by a Legal Practice Course and a further period of recognised training, had kept him interested and occupied for several years. It had, of course, also kept him impoverished and burdened with student loans for which he was now obliged to work in order to repay. Life was proving harsh for her beloved son whose sense of justice was what drove him to both understand and help underprivileged people. In many ways he had been disadvantaged himself; his father having died when he was very young and his much older sister having emigrated to be with the love of her life in Australia. He had been a lonely, introverted child for whom his mother had not had much time since she had also worked long hours in several menial jobs in order to pay the bills. Nevertheless, she loved him and it pained her to see him distressed now.

Louise had been very unkind, in her opinion. Did she not see how hard Arthur had been working? It seemed that nothing was enough to satisfy the girl. Arthur had provided her with a beautiful, if small, home, a similarly small car and a pair of rather large boxer dogs that she had insisted would fill the gap that their childlessness had created. His selfish wife did not go out to work; she fiddle-faddled around with her 'creative' projects in the cabin that Arthur had built for her as a workshop and sometimes, when she felt inclined, she took her finished items to local markets or car boot sales or advertised them on her cheap website. She only really made enough money to buy replacement supplies in order to sustain her crafting and never made a worthwhile profit. How she thought she was going to be able to support herself, Mrs Lancer had no idea.

Arthur had arrived late one evening a few weeks ago. He had been upset, angry and utterly confused. He carried nothing but a tatty holdall; the very same one he had taken to Oxford many years before, which now held some clean clothes, pyjamas, a toothbrush and razor, a sheaf of papers from the office and a well chewed dog toy that had been unintentionally scooped up with the rest of his meagre belongings. "She wants a separation," was all he muttered as his mother let him in. She, holding back tears and questions, held him tight for a moment or two and then replied with, "I'll go up and air the bed in the spare room." And that was how it happened. Never ones for long or deep conversations, the story came out slowly and piecemeal. Louise wanted to travel, she wanted to visit Mary in Australia, she wanted more money, she wanted prestige and a bigger house, she wanted... and she was dissatisfied with life, with her home, with the dogs, the car and with Arthur and she refused to acknowledge his efforts to provide for her, "You're better off without her!" remarked his mother, but Arthur had just looked at her with

17

his dark ringed and saucer-like eyes, "I love her," was all he said.

~

The coffee served to revive his flagging spirits and when it was followed by Amy timidly opening his door to offer him two things; a fresh croissant and the information that his client had been delayed and had remade her appointment for the following day, he actually smiled at her and graciously accepted both. At least he would have time to read the file properly now and since he had only one other appointment for today which was not until five o'clock, he would also have time to sort out the car and maybe even get the bicycle tyres repaired. He picked up the phone and dialled the number of Manston Service and Repairs.

The small market town of Manston was surprisingly well served for almost everything one could require on a day to day basis. Although there were none of the major outlets such as Screw Fix or Toys R Us, other smaller businesses provided similar commodities albeit at a slightly inflated price. Nevertheless, the convenience of having things to hand outweighed the expense of travelling further afield in order to acquire a cheaper model. Set in the rural Miltonshire countryside it had an ambience all of its own which was a combination of a genteel, churchgoing, close knit community and down-to-earth farmers and mildly bohemian youngsters. The whole was tied together with an extremely strong sense of identity and belonging;

once a Manstonian, always included. This however, had a downside in that it took many years for a newcomer to earn the status of automatic inclusion. Percival Arthur Lancer had lived and worked in the town for almost fifteen years and although he was well known, liked and respected he was still referred to as the new partner in the law firm of which he was now the sole active associate. It was, to all intents and purposes, his business since the only remaining partner had retired in all but name three years previously. Barnes and Son was emblazoned on the windows and the polished door plaque listed the incumbents as J Barnes Snr LLB, R Barnes Jnr LLB and PA Lancer (with no letters.) Jonah Barnes had died many years ago and Roger Barnes, now in his late seventies, had retired soon after Arthur had arrived. No one had ever seen reason to alter the window or door plaque and so they remained misleadingly unaltered.

Chapter 3

Partington Hall

"What is so terrifying about change?" a disembodied voice yelled rhetorically to no one in particular. The outburst was followed by a resounding crash and an unrepeatable swear word, a distinct silence and soon after by footsteps clunking up a wooden staircase. The cellar door slammed open and immediately bounced off the wall and closed again, equally noisily but allowing just enough time for the slim figure to emerge carrying a large cardboard box. The box dropped to the kitchen floor as the grubby figure fell back against the now, fortunately perhaps, closed door. An arm, encased in a flimsy sleeve was wiped across a sweaty forehead, serving only to smear the dusty cobwebs further into her already tangled hair. "Oh, for goodness sake, this place will be the death of me!" she exclaimed in exasperation.

"Is that you?" called a querulous voice from somewhere else.

"Who the hell do you think it is?" muttered Amy under her breath before calling, "Yes Mum," as brightly as she could, hopefully disguising her irritation, "Don't worry, nothing is broken and I am fine. I'll be up with your tray in a moment or two."

"Don't forget the albums I asked you to find," came the ungrateful and domineering reply.

Amy bit her tongue and managed to avoid the retort that attempted to escape her lips. Hadn't she almost killed herself in her efforts to find the damn albums? What on earth her mother hoped to discover amongst the dusty relics, she had no idea but find them she had and now she would dust them off, locate a new box and take them up to the bedridden woman in the hope that they would occupy her for the rest of the weekend so that she, Amy, could have a little respite from her mother's never-ending demands.

Grace Murdock had once been a very active member of society. She had always been a busybody and liked to be the centre of attention in every area of her life. She couldn't bear to let other people take the lead and she had to be in control of absolutely any situation or activity she undertook. There was no doubt however, that she had been good at leading, organising and encouraging people to do their duty although her technique, which at times bordered on blackmail, left a great deal to be desired.

The village community had certainly been shocked, if not a little relieved, when the accident had happened. Grace had loved to ride horses. It was her one indulgence in an otherwise austere and regulated routine. In her youth she had owned three horses and indeed the stables still existed in the yard behind Partington Hall although they now housed Amy's car, a couple of bicycles and an assortment of broken tools and household furniture waiting for... who knew!

However, the horse she had been riding on the eventful day had belonged to a neighbour who was away on business. Grace had offered to exercise the rather large cob and despite being warned of his tendency to buck she had waived aside her neighbour's suggestion that she groom and lead the horse rather than mount him. Not having ridden for some time and failing to take into account the increased volume of traffic passing through the country lanes, she had not realised the power of the beast or her own age-related loss of strength in her arms and legs. The oversized lorry that raced past them at breakneck speed spooked the big gelding who took off across a stubbled cornfield at a rate of knots. Grace could not control him and this loss of command led directly to her ultimate loss of power over most aspects of her former life. In many ways it was a sad ending to a fulsome existence; to be deposited unceremoniously in a ditch. To be found several hours later by an excited terrier and its astonished walker and to be carted off to the city in an ambulance with lights flashing and siren blaring, was demeaning and embarrassing for that proud lady. Sadder still was the knowledge that she would not only not ride again, but could not walk unaided and could not therefore, participate in the numerous activities that she had previously... enjoyed? And the loss of her independence was something with which she would never come to terms.

Thank goodness for Amy, that daughter whom she had never really wanted; had never expected to have and who had disappointed her in her inability to be just like her mother. Amy had been conceived in a moment of weakness, liberally lubricated with champagne, shortly after the celebration of her parents' fifteenth wedding anniversary. Grace had been astonished to find herself pregnant at the age of forty-six and dismayed at her husband's concurrent diagnosis of lung cancer. Howard, already a weak, easily dominated man, had lived long enough to see his daughter's fifth birthday. He had doted on her and she, who adored him, was devastated when he was suddenly gone from her world. No one had explained to her why he had disappeared; everyone assumed she was too young to notice or to understand. Her nanny, heaven forbid that Grace should care for her own child, was kindness itself although a simple woman who did as she was told but little more; perfectly suited as far as Grace was concerned. And so Amy grew up learning to be a good girl, to keep out of the way of her unpredictable mother and to do as she was told when she couldn't avoid the telling. Nevertheless, she had a sweet nature and loved to be alone; at first with her dolls and her books, and later with her few friends from school and her dog. The dog, however, was never allowed in the house and the friends were far too afraid of her frightful mother to ever accept any invitation to visit. Not knowing anything different, Amy was happy enough although sometimes rather lonely.

Nowadays there were times when Amy ached for that very loneliness. Her mother's demanding and needful condition meant that apart from her tenuous jobs, when the agency could find something suitable and which fitted around her mother's requirements, she had precious little time to herself and even when the occasional times manifested themselves, she was too exhausted to take advantage of the opportunities and often simply slept instead. Day and night, she was on duty at her mother's beck and call; lifting her onto the commode, emptying the commode, fetching this, fetching that, making her meals, plumping her pillows and generally fulfilling the million and one missions her mother thought up. Despite the installation of a stair lift and two wheelchairs, one upstairs and an electric one downstairs, Grace generally preferred to depend on her daughter for her mobility, almost as though it was her right to be waited on hand and foot. On top of everything else was the general maintenance and running of the ridiculously large house. At least her father had ensured that money was not an issue and although she could well afford not to seek employment, she needed the small freedoms that the duties and the salary allowed for. She liked Arthur Lancer, not in a romantic sense, but he was down to earth, kind and not particularly demanding. Above all, he seemed to appreciate her efforts to please. Neither of them smiled very often but yesterday he had smiled at her and looked much younger than she had thought him to be and when she smiled back, he had noticed her dimples and the sparkle in her eyes.

Sighing to herself, she continued to dust off the old photograph albums, made up the breakfast tray, let the dog out (she was used to sneaking him in at night) and took it all upstairs to her mother.

A little later, having ensured that Grace had to hand everything she might need for the morning, she bade her farewell with a perfunctory kiss on her forehead and a promise to be home at lunchtime. In reply she received a grunt and a head turned away from her attempting to smile face. It was with a heavy heart that she, in her small car with soft music soothing her soul, set off to the office and was more than half way there before her spirits began to lift. She remembered the important appointment for which Arthur had asked her to be early, in case he too was held up again and whilst checking that she was in good time, she idly wondered, what was so important about this particular client?

Chapter 4

The Manse

He knew that he should not. He knew he was playing with fire. He knew that it would end in disaster. He knew that he could not help himself... Damn the woman!

He had been partially responsible for her arrival in his congregation, having been a member of the interview panel that appointed her. She had more than amply fulfilled the various criteria as dictated by the former incumbent and was extremely well qualified for the position. Thus it was that she was offered and accepted the post of Head-Teacher at the small though well attended school in the village of Hingemont.

The Reverend William Banner had a very good reputation amongst his congregation and was well liked by all. His calm and gentle demeanour, together with his wise and eloquently expressed interpretations of 'God's word', his musical baritone and his ability to empathise with even the most crotchety of parishioners, made him acceptable to all, old and young alike. He always had a smile and kind word for adults and a sweetie in his pocket for the children. He never overstepped the mark in terms of appropriate behaviours and no one would ever have suspected him of wrong doing. How mistaken can people be?

~

Matilda Banner scowled to herself as she struggled to peg the washing on the line while the blustery wind did its best to whisk the sheets from her hands and to drape them over the shrubs at the bottom of her garden. Her mind was not on the task in hand; indeed, washing and drying was about as far from her thoughts as it could be despite the necessity of completing this particular chore. The sheets were not her own. Yesterday she had gone round to old Mrs Springfield's house and, using the key that was 'hidden' in the back porch, she had let herself in and tidied up the house, fired up the old Aga, changed the bedding and left a hot-pot for young Imogen's arrival. The poor girl would have had a long journey and the awful circumstances for her coming would surely have taken their toll too. At least she could help a little.

It was as she was tying back the old gate with a piece of orange twine that she had noticed. There was Bill's battered old Ford making its way noisily homeward down the lane – but from the wrong direction! She was quite sure that he had said he was going to visit Grace at her home, but Partington House was the other side of the village. Perhaps he had called elsewhere as well? It would have been unusual of course since he always made a point of telling her exactly where he was going, when and why. Sometimes she wished that he wouldn't! It almost made her feel as though he didn't trust her and being utterly transparent with her meant that she had to be equally open with him. It wasn't that she had anything to hide but sometimes, just sometimes, she would have liked a little privacy; a space in which to think her own thoughts (which didn't always coincide with Bill's) and to pray her own prayers. Instead she felt that she had to agree with everything he said, every decision he made and to keep track of his comings and goings to ensure they were exactly as he had said they would be.

The scowl and the puzzle that currently creased her brow were for this; should she question him about his strange direction or his whereabouts? If she did, wouldn't it suggest that she doubted his integrity? He had said he was going to visit Grace and she was certain that he had, but... She sighed. Perhaps it would be best to say nothing? She was quite sure there would be a simple explanation. He would tell her when he was ready...

~

Layla stretched luxuriously. She glanced at the bedside clock and breathed deeply as she realised that she could allow herself at least another ten minutes before needing to leave the cosy warmth of her bed. She thought idly of the day ahead, Sunday. The service would begin at eleven but she should be at the Church a good half an hour before then. The children of the choir would need tidying up and dressing in their robes. A quick practise of the psalm and the first line of each hymn wouldn't do any harm too. It was amazing how quickly they forgot their lines! She thought of the children; Sammy, Greg, Tony and Kit and Anna, Jilly, Sophie, Tammy and Meg – would they all attend today? These were the eldest children in the school and it was their privilege to provide the church choir. A dubious privilege for some but it was a long-standing tradition of the village and one she was happy to encourage. Especially now...

She knew that most of them would come but she worried about little Sammy. She wasn't sure what the problems were but she realised that life wasn't always straightforward for the solemn little boy. Much of the time he was alone but she often saw him on the edge of the crowd of other children with a look of longing in his eyes. He was a little thin and often pale faced but he seemed healthy enough and he had an obvious affinity with animals. She sometimes watched him leaving the school yard and noticed that regularly he was met by a tabby cat and sometimes a black and white collie dog that obviously adored him and greeted him rapturously. He had said that when he grew up, he wanted to be a vet but the truth was that she very much doubted his academic ability. Perhaps it was wrong to judge when the child was so enthused but she didn't want to raise his expectations just to have them dashed when it came to the crunch. Last Friday, after each child had been invited to say what they thought they'd like to become in adulthood, she had suggested to him, gently of course, that he might like to consider something different. She was sorry that the resulting upset had caused him to slam out of the schoolroom at the end of the day with angry tears coursing down his cheeks. Sometimes it was so hard to do the right thing...

Layla stretched again, threw back the covers and padded to the bathroom. She peeled off her flimsy nightdress and admired her slender body in the long mirror. She smiled to herself as, Sammy temporarily forgotten, she remembered and a tingle of excitement flushed her cheeks in anticipation and for the secrecy of it all which made it so much more... dangerous?

~

Damn the woman! Again, The Rev Bill swore to himself. She was just too perfect, too tempting and utterly irresistible. He felt himself stir underneath his cassock and took a deep breath in order to control his mind and body.

The service had been well attended, his sermon appreciated and Mattie had gone back to the Manse to cook the lunch – Sunday roast of course. He pulled off his stole, kissed it and folded it carefully before removing his robe and putting it back on its hanger in the small wardrobe in the vestry. He said a brief prayer and was just about to leave the room when suddenly she was there. She flung her arms around his neck and kissed him passionately. He didn't want to respond but his body dictated otherwise until he pushed her roughly from him and pinned her arms by her sides. "Not now," he muttered gruffly, "I have to go home now." She pouted a little but realising the truth of his situation, she kissed him lightly on the cheek saying, "Later then?"

"Maybe..." he replied.

Chapter 5

Hingemont House

She sat in the bay window of the old-fashioned lounge. The sun shone weakly but was enough to warm her face and neck as the mug that she cradled warmed her hands. The wind had been cold but at least yesterday's constant downpour had abated and the ground had not been too muddy although Benjy had certainly needed a wash before he was allowed further than the kitchen and definitely not on the furniture.

Imogen had begun her day early. Despite it being a Sunday and there being no particular purpose to pursue, she found herself wide awake at six o'clock. She supposed that her earlier than usual bedtime and the long journey yesterday had meant that her sleep was deep and consequently she woke rested and energetic. Her first thought had been to let her loved ones know that all was well. After some irritation and frustrating lack of signal, she had eventually sent the message. By leaning as far out of the turret window as she could, she finally heard a satisfying 'ping' that told her the text had been sent. Her safe arrival and the lack of any information so far to pass on to her invalid Mother, her brothers and her cousins, would be circulated by Aunt Millie, the only one of her relatives to regularly check her messages.

She made herself a cup of tea and found a loaf of bread for toast and still it was only seven a.m. Not having anything that she had to do, and unable to relax, even before the sun was fully up, she had donned her walking boots, a warm coat and scarf and while most of the villagers were still in bed, she and a rather surprised Benjy could be seen striding across the bridleway towards the next village.

Making a sharp turn to the right when she came to a cross-path, she found herself nearing St Mary's Church. It had not been her intention to visit the site so soon but here she was and it seemed silly to turn away before she had assessed for herself where it had happened.

~

She didn't know the full story of course. The message had been a bit garbled and it hadn't come to her directly. Mum had received a phone call; she couldn't recall exactly who it was from, but she was very upset and almost incoherent when she rang Imogen.

"It's Gran," she had sobbed, "you have to go and see what's to do…"

"What's happened, Mum?" Imogen was trying to make sense of her mother's words.

"I don't know what has happened but it's something bad. There's a number you can ring. They said anytime would be alright."

"Who are they?"

"I don't know, I just don't know…" more sobs and some indecipherable mumblings,

"Ok Mum, just give me the number. Please calm down and I'll try to find out what's going on. Then I'll come and see you."

An hour or so later, after a very unsatisfactory telephone conversation with some low-ranking police official who was reluctant to give any information to anyone other than her mother, despite assurances that she was in no fit state to either visit or receive visitors, Imogen was really none the wiser. All she knew was that Gran had been found dead, in the churchyard. How, when, why or any other detail were only to be imparted to her in person, in Manton, as soon as she could present herself at the offices of J. Barnes and Son. She was somewhat puzzled as to why she should receive the particulars from a lawyer; surely the police would be the ones to provide such information?

As promised, Imogen went to her mother. She comforted her as she told her the little that she knew, reassured her as best she could and promised to keep her in the picture as soon as there was anything to impart. She spoke briefly to the nursing staff at the home where her mother now lived and they assured Imogen that they would keep an eye on her mother and sedate her if necessary. Alzheimer's is such a cruel disease. Imogen's Mum was only sixty-two but already she was forgetful and at times very childish in her behaviours. Recently, it had become increasingly clear that she could no longer look after herself and so Imogen and her brothers had arranged for her to move into Sundown Nursing Home. It was a pleasant place with residents ranging from three young mentally disabled people to some very elderly and frail ladies and gentlemen. Mum seemed happy enough and the nursing staff were kind and patient. It goes without saying that no one had expected it to be Mum who would need that sort of care and everyone had assumed that, in time, Gran would. How things change when you least expect it!

~

Her visit to the churchyard had told her precisely nothing. All was tidy, no one was there and all Imogen had was a long list of questions to put to the lawyer the following morning. She sighed as she untangled her legs and crossed the room to return her empty mug to the kitchen. She would need to think about going shopping perhaps; there didn't seem to be much in the larder although she hadn't looked in the big freezer yet. Gran would surely have had some provisions hidden away somewhere? Unlike her mum, Gran was still very much compos mentis and despite her age, until more recently she had regularly driven herself to the supermarket and to church as well as to the various clubs and meetings that she enjoyed. Nowadays, her shopping was done by bus or taxi but she still insisted on her independence. None of this new-fangled online shopping for her! She was a busy person and liked to be involved in all that was available to her; at least, she had been...

Imogen wiped a tear from her cheek. Of course, she had known that Gran couldn't live forever, she was eighty-eight after all, but for her ending to have come so suddenly and in such a way... she had to find out the truth... Perhaps she would go to the Church service this morning? She glanced at her wristwatch, there was plenty of time. Service was at ten-thirty and it was still only nine-forty-five. She felt better for having made a decision and so she quickly tidied her hair, washed her face, changed her shoes, shut Benjy in the lobby, and set off. She still arrived early!

Chapter 6

Partington Hall

Monday had been a difficult day and Amy was relieved to finally be home albeit rather later than usual. She had made a brief visit at lunchtime as promised, but had found her mother asleep, the photo album upside down on the floor and the breakfast tray balanced precariously on the bedside table. She had righted the album and removed the tray, let Pip out into the garden to relieve himself and replenished the tray with a flask of soup and a crusty cheese roll for Grace's lunch. She wouldn't wake her mother for fear of her making further demands that would delay her previously unplanned return to the office for a few hours. Pip had disappeared into the shrubbery at the bottom of the large garden and so she reluctantly left him outside. There was a kennel in which he could shelter and the garden was secure provided she remembered to shut and fasten the gate.

Usually, at this time of day, mid afternoon, Grace would be watching the small television that was attached to the wall in her bedroom and operated by a remote-control device, but today, the first thing that Amy had noticed, once she had pacified the excited Pip, was the silence. Perhaps her mother had fallen asleep again? She was just about to put the kettle on to make some tea, when a sound startled her. At first it was just a sort of scuffling noise as though something was being dragged across the floor upstairs, but this was quickly followed by a loud thump and a cry of anguish. Amy fled up the stairs, bumping her hip against the recently installed stair-lift, stumbling in her haste, and flung open her mother's bedroom door. She gasped, "What on earth… Mum, what are you doing?"

"Don't stand there gawping girl, help me up!" Grace barked her order in her usual irascible manner. However, much to Amy's surprise, she suddenly dissolved into tears; great heartrending sobs that wracked her frail body as she buried her face in her arms where they lay on the carpeted floor. Amy knelt beside her mother. Astonished by this uncharacteristic display of emotion, she was at a loss as to what to say or do but instinct told her to wait, to let her mother's grief at whatever it was that troubled her, to run its course as it surely would.

As her sobbing began to abate, although her shoulders still heaved in great shudders as she struggled to compose herself, Amy gently lifted her mother from her prone position and carefully eased her into the armchair that waited by the window. She tucked a fleecy rug around Grace's thin shoulders and across her knees before hurrying downstairs to finish making the pot of tea. She knew better than to quiz her mother while she was still distressed; she would learn soon enough what had prompted this unusual occurrence.

~

As she prepared the brew, a task that needed little in the way of thought or concentration, she thought back to the unusual events of the day at work. It was rare that Arthur asked her to return after lunch but today there were some important papers to be prepared following his morning appointment. There was some apparent mystery over this affair and everything was rather hush-hush so, apart from the details to which she had been privy; a coroner's report and a statement from the attending police officer, she really didn't know any more of what it was all about.

This much she did know; old Mrs Springfield, from Hingemont House, had been found dead in St Mary's churchyard. The coroner's initial finding suggested that her death was from a blow to the head. There were no witnesses and despite a few suspicious circumstances, such as a blood-stained rock which was lying near the body and an emptied handbag flung into the hedgerow, there was no indication as to how the old lady had come to be lying in a pool of her own blood. She had apparently been found by Charlie, the simple chap who looked after the churchyard, who had been cutting the grass on the far side of the Church. Later, in his statement he would claim that while making his way round to the small store shed to put away his tools, he had seen the prone figure. At the time, his hysterical yells had alerted a passer-by who, realising his distress but not the cause, telephoned the police before hurrying away; not wanting to become involved in anything untoward. The young police-woman who attended as soon as she could, her only form of transport being her horse, found the agitated groundsman brandishing a blood-stained shovel and with more blood on his hands and overalls. She had cautioned him and told him that he would be expected to make a statement in due course. No doubt Amy would also be asked to prepare whatever he provided for the forthcoming enquiry.

Hingemont was normally such a quiet and unprepossessing place with not much going on at all! She felt sorry for the poor girl, Ada Springfield's grand-daughter, who had come all this way to find out what had happened. She seemed nice. Perhaps she should invite her for coffee or to go for a walk – she thought she remembered mention of a dog. It would do Pip good to have a companion once in a while...

~

The tea prepared and some biscuits found, Amy made her way cautiously back upstairs. It was always a little awkward negotiating the stair-lift, but generally she had developed a technique for avoiding bumping her thigh and slopping the tea. A rapidly forming bruise reminded her to be extra cautious this time. She found her mother, still sniffing, but largely composed, with her eyes closed

40

and a bereft look on her face. Amy felt a surge of compassion for her mother. It must be so very hard for her now that she had lost most of her independence and it was all too easy to feel resentful of her demands. She put the tray down carefully and placing a hand on Grace's shoulder, "Mum," she whispered, "are you awake?"

A vigorous sniff affirmed and Grace's eyes flickered open. Red rimmed and still tearful but largely controlled, she managed a weak smile before saying gruffly, "Sorry. Have you brought the tea?"

~

A little while later, back in the kitchen, Amy puzzled over mother's distress. She was aware that Grace and Ada Springfield had known each other and she knew that theirs had been a somewhat stormy friendship but she hadn't realised just how upsetting the whole unfortunate affair had been for her mum. At the time, Grace had seemed to accept that it was 'just one of those things' and had shrugged off Amy's conciliatory words but now she was apparently blaming herself! What on earth could she have had to do with Ada's terrible accident?

Chapter 7

Manton

The small market town was busy. Monday morning and it was raining. Parking had been difficult and Imogen had walked into the town centre from the riverside car park. Her wet umbrella was propped in the corner of the small café where she sipped her cappuccino and idly crumbled the biscuit that had been balanced on the ridiculously small saucer. Benjy would have enjoyed the crumbs had she not been obliged to leave him behind this time. The appointment was for nine forty-five but, determined not to be late, she had arrived far too early. Hence the coffee and a wait, whilst watching the world and his wife hurry past the window. Perhaps that was a slight exaggeration – the town was busy, but in comparison to her flat in Walthamstow which was always chaotic and noisy, it was really quite subdued and quiet. People were hurrying to work and the persistent rain meant that heads were down, hoods were up and nobody stopped for a quick chat or to respond to their mobile phone's pings; all of which contributed to the illusion of busyness. Imogen sighed and took another sip of her cooling coffee. She checked the time on the Church clock opposite where she was sitting in the window of the café and realised with a start that it still said nine fifteen as it had shortly after she arrived. Hastily she took out her phone and checked; nine thirty-six! This time she sighed with relief, drank the rest of the beverage and pulled on her damp coat. She raised her hand to thank the young waitress, grabbed her umbrella and set off up the high street to the office she had first visited last week.

That visit had been somewhat surprising and she still wasn't too sure what to make of the situation. The first account of her grandmother's demise had suggested that she had experienced an unfortunate accident in the churchyard but now there seemed to be some suggestion that it had been no accident at all.

Not wanting to prejudice Imogen's perception of the due processes, the investigating officer had decided that it would be more appropriate for her to be kept informed by her grandmother's lawyer, Arthur Lancer. He was unlikely to be involved in the enquiries and could therefore give her an impartial report as things progressed and advise her if and when such advice should become necessary. There would be some delay before the body could be released for whatever form of disposal was decided upon, which would give the girl time to inform the rest of Mrs Springfield's relations; and there was the question of the Will.

Arthur had been quite sure that Mrs Springfield's Will was lodged in her file with all her other official documents, but despite his search, ably assisted by Amy, they had been unable to find it. This was the main reason for Imogen's visit today. He needed to ask her to search at Hingemont House; it seemed likely that Ada had taken it home after her visit a month or so ago. She had asked to see it and had mentioned some revisions that she wanted to make. Arthur thought that she had returned it by post but he may have been mistaken. He knew that her estate was quite large; probably larger than anyone actually realised and so it was important that things were dealt with in the appropriate manner...

"Of course I'll look for it," it went without saying that she would, "but can you tell me a little more about what happened?" Imogen felt uncomfortable and slightly tearful – she couldn't explain why exactly, except that the thought of her grandmother being murdered was really rather alarming. Why would anyone want to kill her lovely Gran?

"I don't know very much about it," began Arthur, "but I understand that your grandmother's car keys were missing as was her mobile phone." Ada Springfield's mobile phone was extremely ancient. She had owned it ever since her daughter Millie had insisted on her obtaining one. She may have used it half a dozen times but it really wasn't something of which she made regular use.

Arthur continued, "Her handbag and empty wallet were found under a hedge about a mile away, towards Luttington, but the car was nowhere to be seen and the phone hasn't been used since that day. You must understand that it's all a bit suspicious and so the police feel that they cannot rule out foul play. An opportunist perhaps who hit her with the rock – you remember the blood stains I mentioned?" Imogen nodded and he continued, "Someone knocked her out – or at least thought that's what they had done, and then took her bag, stole the car and flung away the bits that were of no use to whoever it was."

"I suppose that sounds plausible," Imogen sounded doubtful, "but in Hingemont? It's always so quiet with hardly anyone around during the day...?"

"There have been a few reports of unsavoury looking characters hanging about the village green," replied Arthur, "in particular, an influx of foreign workers at the fruit farm in Layton. The farmer there has brought them in to help with the harvest." Imogen remembered seeing the soggy notice announcing the forthcoming Harvest Festival. She nodded again, "Well, I suppose the police know what they're doing but I do hope they hurry up. Of course, we want to know what happened to Gran..." she sniffed tearfully and Arthur passed her a conveniently placed tissue box, "... but really, we just want to be able to say goodbye properly. Will I be allowed to see her...? I mean see her body?"

A short while later, arrangements having been made with the coroner's office for Imogen to see her grandmother the following Friday afternoon,

Amy handed her a slip of paper with the Mortuary address written in neat rounded letters. Just as Imogen was about to leave the reception area, Amy held out another note, "This is my phone number and address. I live on the outskirts of the village not too far from your gran's place," she hesitated, "I know it might seem a bit presumptuous but I wondered if you might like to come for coffee or to take the dogs out? I have a little terrier, Pip, and I think I overheard you mention that you have a dog too?" Imogen smiled, it was nice to think she might have someone she could talk to, really talk, not all this official stuff! "How kind," she said, "I'd like that very much! Maybe tomorrow?"

"Yes, that would be great," Amy beamed at her, "I'll be home by one o'clock and as soon as I've prepared lunch for Mum we could walk if this rain has stopped. If not, we'll pop into the little restaurant at the garden centre; we can chat there for as long as we like!"

The two girls smiled at each other and with a little wave, Imogen left feeling much lighter and more optimistic than she had since she left home. Was it really only a week ago that she had arrived to find herself in the middle of this mess?

It was considerably later when Imogen, recounting by a telephone call to her brother her conversation with Arthur Lancer, realised, with something of a shock, what he had said about car keys. She was sure she remembered being told that Gran had given up driving some time ago... why then would she have had car keys in her pocket or her handbag and how would anyone have known they were missing? There were beginning to be rather a lot of things that just didn't add up and Imogen wondered more and more, what on earth had happened to Gran?

Chapter 8

Sammy

It wasn't fair! What right did she have to tell him what he could or couldn't be? He always knew he was going to be a vet – what else could he be? No one understands him like the animals do and no one understands the animals like he does. So, it stands to reason that he will become a vet...

Sammy scowled behind the book he was supposed to be reading. It was a boring book about boring people; there were no animals and no pictures. Some of the words were long and difficult and he had no idea what it was supposed to be about. Now if it had a dog or a cat in it, or even a cow or an elephant, then it might be more interesting – but it didn't and it wasn't!

"Sammy, stop rocking your chair, it'll tip over backwards and you'll bang your head!" Now there's a thought! Perhaps that would get him out of the classroom for the rest of the day? Miss Lester was suddenly beside his desk with her hand firmly on the back of his chair, forcing him to return the front legs to the floor but banging his elbows on the desk top in the process. Tears sprang to his eyes but he wasn't going to let her see them. "Why are you not reading the section I identified?" she asked. Taking the book roughly from his hands, she opened it at the appointed page and pointed to the paragraph he was supposed to have read. The other children sniggered; Sammy was in trouble again. Sammy hated Miss Lester!

Layla Lester had arrived at St Mary's village school only a year ago after the previous incumbent had retired after more than thirty years as head teacher. Although she was an experienced teacher, this was her first appointment as head of a school, and of working in such a small school too. The twenty-one pupils were distributed in two classes, one for the infants (up to age seven) and the other for the older children before they moved on to the private upper school in Wendle or the state secondary in Manton. Mrs Postlethwaite had been the infant teacher for almost as long as the former head and no one could imagine the school without her smiling, rotund presence. Nevertheless, she had her doubts about the flibbertigibbet young woman who had begun to try to change things from how they had always been – 'progress' she called it! Not only that but she seemed to have caught the eye of the vicar too. Pamela Postlethwaite had seen their heads together, ostensibly discussing the forthcoming Harvest Festival, but the looks that passed between them were suggestive of more than a working partnership. She wouldn't pass judgement just yet. Time would tell and being the kind-hearted and optimistic natured woman that she was, no one would be permitted to think Pamela a gossip monger.

"It's not fair!" Sammy opined to his mother who retorted that life isn't fair and he might as well get used to it.

"It's not fair!" Sammy grumbled to his dad who absently asked him what wasn't fair and why did he expect anything to be fair?

"It's not bloody fair!" Sammy shouted to no one in particular but his granny told him off for swearing. He slammed out of the door and ran down the road to his favourite place in the nearby Ashford Forest. He wasn't really supposed to go there since it was a private estate but he knew how to wriggle through the fence and had built himself a small hide in amongst the undergrowth. From there he could watch the birds and the wildlife and he took delight in seeing the Roe deer and the badgers, the squirrels and the pheasants that roamed freely in the safety of the large enclosed areas. Here he could forget about the iniquities of life and especially the unfairness of Miss Lester.

Miss Lester should more properly be addressed as Mrs Lester since she had been married to John Lester for at least nine years. Recently divorced from her wayward husband she had thought that the move to the remote village of Hingemont would provide the salve her damaged heart and pride desired. She had not expected anything more than a welcome from the villagers and had assumed that her position as head of the school would mean that she was instantly accepted into the small close-knit community. How wrong could she have been? Not long after her arrival she was made aware of the difficulties of infiltrating the cliques and friendship groups that had built up over many years. Even Pamela Postlethwaite had tried to warn her that it would take time for her to be accepted as anything other than an outsider. How true her words had become!

The only person who had shown her any sort of welcome, other than the formalities of the teacher/parent relationship, had been Reverend Banner or Bill as she had come to think of him. He had welcomed her musicality and had immediately handed over responsibility for the small church choir which was mostly made up of the older school children, two or three ladies from the village, the Reverend himself and Charlie the groundsman. Rehearsals were intermittent with most of the practicing being done in music lessons at school and the occasional Sunday morning before an early service. During these rehearsals the ladies would chatter to each other, only stopping when the singing began, and paid little heed to how Layla directed them. They had sung the hymns and psalms many, many times and knew them by heart. Any attempt at innovation or change was met with stony faces and muttered grumbles about 'new-fangled ideas' or 'modern music' and 'what's wrong with the way we've always done it?' Layla had almost given up hope but Bill insisted that they would accept her eventually and that she should persist in her attempts to liven up the services before the church lost its entire congregation and, in consequence, he his job.

She hadn't meant to develop feelings for him but it was very hard to resist his kindness when all about her were giving her the cold shoulder and encouraging her to wonder whether she should stay in this unwelcoming place.

He hadn't meant to develop feelings for her, he loved his wife. Mattie was a good woman. No longer the vibrant exciting girl he had fallen in love with, in her maturity she was more rounded both in figure and in nature and her sadness at not being able to have children had put an inevitable distance between them. Nevertheless, he would never have deliberately hurt her and he had no intention of letting this 'fling', as he dismissively labelled it, do anything other than re-charge his flagging libido and lift his dampened spirits. Mattie would be grateful for his renewed interest in her femininity and perhaps Layla could teach him a few tricks with which to pleasure his wife. Foolish and short-sighted? Perhaps... but then you never know how someone else will react to your own self reasoning.

After the first time he had felt both exhilarated and ashamed. He hadn't meant for it to happen and he didn't think that she had either. They had arranged to meet to discuss the hymns for the following Sunday service and somehow, she had tripped as she was entering the vestry. He had caught her in his arms, caught the scent of her perfume mixed with the unmistakable scent of her womanhood and before he had stopped to consider, he had kissed her pouting lips. She had responded unresistingly and the rest was history. Once begun, neither could nor wanted to stop and so since that time they had met fairly regularly, always discreetly and, as far as they knew, no one had any idea as to what was going on.

But Sammy knew! That is, he knew that something was going on but not exactly what! He hadn't seen anything that he shouldn't but he had seen them together, many times...

Chapter 9

Layton Farm

Layton Farm had an excellent reputation for fine fruit and vegetables. Housed in the big barn was a farm shop which was well used by the local villagers and by people from further afield since prices were reasonable and quality exceptional.

This success inevitably led to more planting, more harvesting and consequently more need for workers to pick and sort the produce, not only for the home market but also for shipping out to many of the major supermarket chains in the nearby towns and cities. Thus it was that, particularly in the summer and autumn months, many foreigners were employed by Farmer Franklin who had advertised on the World Wide Web for 'Strong and Willing' people to bring in the harvest. Unbeknownst to him, since he spent as little time behind his computer as was absolutely necessary, his advertisement had sparked considerable interest in several overseas communities and a band of somewhat disadvantaged and non-English speaking individuals had been gathered together by a smaller group of disreputable scoundrels who were intent on exploiting their ignorance for personal gain. In due course, the motley crew arrived and were set to work. Willing and able as required they worked diligently despite the promised ten pounds per hour being reduced by the manipulative rogues to seven pounds fifty. Nevertheless, this still represented riches indeed for the poor who were unaware that the extra had been creamed off and found its way into the pockets of the crooked organisers.

Otto Vasovich was grateful for the opportunity. Not only had it meant that he could leave the poverty of his Lithuanian village, but he had also been able to send a small sum of money home to help his elderly and sickly mother. The paltry sum that he had sent would have meant nothing to you or me but it had enabled his mother to buy much needed medicines and a warm coat for the winter. She very much hoped that he would send more...

Otto had been warned once or twice for his indolence. He had always found it hard to leave his bed in the mornings and here, with the heavy, back-breaking work, the long hours and the meagre food supplied, it had become even harder. Thierry had said that his pay would be docked for every minute late that he appeared for breakfast but on that particular morning he had awoken with a terrible headache, a burning desire to urinate and an overwhelming thirst. If he had not needed to pee, he didn't think that he would have left his bed at all. Pulling on his work trousers and jacket, he stumbled out of the log cabin which served as a dormitory for the workers and headed for the washroom.

When he eventually made it into the cafeteria, almost everyone else had finished eating and were making their way to the various fields, polytunnels and packing sheds. Thierry, who was leaning against the serving counter and sipping the last dregs of his mug of coffee, took one look at Otto and sent him back to bed saying, "Merde! That'll be a whole day's pay for you, young man, and no breakfast either!" There was no sympathy, either in his voice or his expression and despite not fully understanding the words spoken, although the meaning was clear, Otto wondered to himself why the foreman had to be so harsh. Perhaps he'd been treated badly himself and so deemed it necessary to punish everyone else for his own circumstances. It was in Otto's nature to be magnanimous but Thierry seemed to manage to push everyone to their utmost limit. Grabbing a large glassful of water, Otto made his way shakily back to the dormitory. He drank deeply and threw himself, fully clothed, onto the bed and in no time at all was once more asleep.

Several hours later, he woke again and finding his headache gone and his hunger renewed, he tidied his rumpled clothes and decided to make the most of his unexpected holiday. He would take a walk in the weak autumnal sunshine and explore the little village he had noticed on the outer edges of the field where he had been working during the previous week. He did not want to go towards where the work was being done that day in case Thierry saw him and considered him fit to work after all. And so it was that he made his way towards the village of Hingemont and the discovery that would alter the path of the next few weeks and possibly the rest of his life.

~

He couldn't decide whether the hard slab of a bed in the cell was better or worse than the bunk in the cabin dormitory. However, he was grateful for the isolation and warmth the cell provided. He had not enjoyed the noisy chatter of the other men who shared the cabin and nor did he appreciate the laughter and high-pitched squeals of the women in the room next door. Why was it that a group of young women always seemed to find so much to talk about? And why were they incapable of speaking in hushed tones – except on the rare occasions when you actually wanted to hear what they had to say! The cell he now found himself locked in, provided an oasis of peace and quiet despite the fact that he didn't understand why he had been arrested and incarcerated there. There was no doubt that he should have taken more interest in his English lessons at school! He had certainly learned a few new words and phrases in his short time here but he really hadn't made much sense of the angry words spoken to him by the burly and very irate police officer who handcuffed him and bundled him into the back of the van that had chased him through winding lanes.

Of course, he knew he had done wrong. He shouldn't have 'borrowed' the car – or taken the money – but the temptation had been too great and he would surely have returned the vehicle from whence he had taken it when his joyride ended. The money? Well, that was another matter – but it hadn't been much and he was sure she could have afforded to lose it. In any case, she certainly hadn't looked as though she was going to need money for quite some time.

Chapter 10

Hingemont House

It seemed that it never stopped raining in this far flung corner of England. Despite an early afternoon break and some weak sunshine during which she had joined Amy for a short walk with Pip and Benjy, Imogen gazed out of the lounge window and watched the growing puddles as they formed a small lake in the centre of the unkempt lawn. She wasn't surprised to see a small flock of seagulls hover hopefully over the hedge but they flew on to more promising and sheltered pastures as the wind lashed the driving rain against the large unsheltered expanse of wall of the old house.

Sighing, she uncurled her cramped legs and stood up. Time to make another call to her brothers and explain what was going on and why there was a delay in making any funeral arrangements. She had enjoyed her walk with Amy who had explained how things seemed to happen much more slowly here in the countryside. "There never seems to be a rush," she said, "until you've got a lot to do. Then everything is wanted yesterday," she laughed. It was a frustrating state of affairs, especially when there was much to be done at home. Her mother might be missing her and there was still the business of sorting out her house and selling her own flat in order to relocate closer to Sundown nursing home and to pay the inordinate fees. The timing for Gran's demise really could not have been much more inconvenient.

Chiding herself for her uncharitable thoughts, she made her way to the old-fashioned telephone in the hallway. Thank goodness Gran had insisted on retaining the landline; no new-fangled mobile phone for her and in any case the signal out here was appalling. Checking her wristwatch, Imogen reassured herself that at least one of her brothers would be at home by this time. Max was an accountant and worked in the City. His hours were irregular and he often attended extravagant meetings and meals in the evenings. Heaven knows how Catherine put up with his erratic comings and goings, but then she wasn't much better herself with her high-flying fashion world commitments. No, it was Archie who should be available for a chat at this time. A geography teacher in a local comprehensive, Archie was usually home soon after 5.00pm and although his childminding duties began at that point, so that Avril could leave for her nursing shift, the children were generally well behaved and glued to the television for a short while.

She dialled the number quickly and was rewarded almost as promptly by a young voice; "Hello, how may I help you?" Carly shrieked with delight when she recognised her Aunty Imogen's voice and the phone clattered to the floor as she ran to find her daddy. By the time Imogen had stopped smiling to herself, Archie's sonorous tones were greeting her and asking her what news. Although she couldn't provide him with much reassurance in terms of further arrangements or details of what had happened to poor Gran, she was able to tell him not to worry about her or Mum. A call to Sundown the previous day had elicited the information that Mum was 'comfortable if confused' which really didn't tell Imogen very much more than she was already aware. The most useful thing that transpired from today's brief conversation was Archie's suggestion as to where she might find the missing document. He remembered being shown by Grandpa, a 'safe' place where the elderly couple kept a fairly significant supply of cash, Gran's jewellery, such as it was, and the deeds to the house, "I should think she may well have put it in there," he suggested. With promises to look from Imogen and assurances to visit Mum from Archie, the call ended with, "Love you," and "Love you too," and an agreed update in a few days' time.

Once she had made herself a fresh mug of tea and had fed Benjy his dinner, she pushed open the door to the small room that had served as Grandpa's study. Originally the Butler's parlour, the room was gloomy and stuffy with only one rather small window which opened onto a walled yard where once the laundry would have been hung to dry. Imogen flicked on the light switch but the dim light that emanated from the cobweb strewn lamp did little to illuminate the dingy space. There was no doubt that the room had not been entered for some considerable time. Dust covered every surface including the numerous boxes and books that cluttered the desk, the chair and the sideboard. There was barely any visible surface that was not encumbered with bric-a-brac and curios; evidence of Grandpa's penchant for collecting 'things'. He could never resist an antique or craft fair and always made some sort of unsuitable purchase in order to 'support the efforts' of those who organised such events. It was one of the very few things that he and Gran had disagreed on and the issue was resolved many years ago by the provision of Grandpa's 'den' in which he was allowed to keep his precious 'finds'.

To the children, in their youth, it had been a wonderful place full of extraordinary objects and the most incredible stories that Grandpa made up about each item. According to him, everything was of fantastic value and he was going to one day make his fortune by selling his treasures, but today, the room was a sorry reminder of his absence and the vanishing of dreams and stories. An aroma of stale pipe tobacco and mould pervaded the room and, had it not been quite so wet outside, Imogen would have flung open the window to try to let in a little fresh air. As it was, she made do with pushing the door as wide as it would go and propped it open with a chair. Benjy, having finished his meal, scuttled between her legs and busied himself sniffing out the inevitably ubiquitous mice and spiders. Imogen shuddered and tried not to imagine just how many creepy crawlies were hiding in there. Realising that at some point she would almost certainly have to go through the daunting prospect of examining every item in the room, she began by focusing on the big old oak desk. There was a large drawer above the knee hole and three vertical smaller drawers on either side. She slid open the top drawer and a small brown mouse scuttled out. A shriek, a chase, a yap and a snap later, the mouse was no more. Benjy was going to have his work cut out in here.

In the drawer were a lot of old bills, statements and letters as well as pens, pencils, rubber bands and paper clips. Nestled at the bottom was a key. Unlocking the fastened columns of drawers, Imogen discovered more of the same sorts of items, including receipts and valuation papers. In the bottom of the final drawer she found some letters tied with what had once been a pink ribbon. Love letters, she assumed and put them on one side to read later on. It felt a little disrespectful to read the endearments her grandparents had exchanged but she was curious to know their history and if she found anything unsavoury, well of course she could just burn the evidence.

It's amazing how easily we can be distracted by our preconceived notions; paperwork would be kept in an office or study; wouldn't it? And it was only after she had been rummaging through the dusty desk for about an hour, that she remembered what Archie had said about the safe place. 'Stupid

girl,' she muttered to herself, 'it's not in here at all!'
Accordingly, she dusted herself down as best she
could and made her way upstairs to Gran's
bedroom. It felt almost intrusive to be entering this
room but in here it was light and airy and clean,
despite the light sprinkling of dust on the dressing
table surface. She would come in here with a duster
tomorrow but first she crossed to the walnut
veneered wardrobe which stood by a matching
tallboy and chest of drawers. Kneeling down she
carefully curled her fingers round the edge of the
kickboard on the bottom right hand side. She found
the slightly loosened joint and by hooking her
thumbnail into a missing screw hole she prised out a
section that had been carefully cut to disguise a
space behind. There lay a shabby red box tied with
a length of pyjama cord that had once been purple
but was now greying and dusty. She eased the box
out from its hiding place and untied the cord. The
box collapsed open revealing its contents; a roll of
bank notes, a pouch of coins, a velvet jewellery box
and, at last, a cardboard document folder.
"Hooray!" she muttered and after carefully
replacing the secret panel, hurried downstairs into
the warmth of the kitchen to examine her finds.

Chapter 11

The Manse

Matilda Banner was troubled. She couldn't really say what it was that worried her but things just didn't feel right and she was the sort of person who relied on instincts and intuition to guide her daily decision-making processes. She had been aware for some time that something had changed but she couldn't pinpoint either what it was or when it had begun to be different. Nevertheless, different it was. As always, her way of dealing with difficulties was too busy herself in domestic activity and this morning she had determined to make a casserole and a cake for that poor girl over at Hingemont House. She must have finished the hot-pot by now and no doubt she was rattling around a bit in the big old house. She remembered seeing her striding across the back meadow with her little dog early one morning and so, when the cooking was ready to be presented to the girl, she slipped into a plastic pot, a few scraps for the dog.

The knock on the door startled Imogen and caused Benjy to bark sharply. A few of the flaking sheets of notepaper fluttered to the floor as she rose to greet whoever had presented themselves at this time. She was both surprised and pleased to see the vicar's wife, food containers clasped to her bosom, smiling and asking if she could come in for a short while. Imogen welcomed her warmly and thanked her profusely for this new offering and for the wonderful food she had so thoughtfully left in readiness for Imogen's arrival last week.

"I had no idea who could have left things so beautifully ready for me," she exclaimed, "and I'm so sorry I didn't phone you to thank you for your thoughtfulness. There's been so much to think about that I'm afraid it simply slipped my mind. Please forgive me?"

Matilda bent to pick up the fallen papers, hiding her uncomfortable pleasure at Imogen's apology. She never expected to be thanked for her efforts to please; it was just part of her role; to provide for others. Isn't that what a clergyman's wife was expected to do? "There's no need to apologise, or to thank me," she murmured, "I'm glad it helped you to feel at home." She fondled Benjy's ears as he wriggled in pleasure at someone else's attention. "I wondered if there was anything else you might need? Anything I can help you with?" Already her feelings of unease and discontent were dissipating as she immersed herself in someone else's potential problems.

"Tell me a bit about Gran's involvement in the village and the church?" asked Imogen, "I don't remember much from when I was here as a child, although we often came to stay. I suppose whatever Gran was doing at that time was put on hold while she had we children to care for and entertain!" She chuckled as she remembered the chaotic, noisy and

66

exciting times she, her brothers and her cousins had enjoyed when staying with her grandparents, "It was always something of a madhouse in those days!"

About an hour later, Matilda could be seen making her way back to the Manse. She was smiling to herself and there was a new lift to her step. Tomorrow she would go back to Hingemont House armed with buckets, dusters, brooms and cleaning paraphernalia in order to help Imogen clean and tidy some of the more neglected areas of the big house and especially her Grandpa's study – oh dear what a terrible mess that was!

Imogen too was feeling lighter and more at ease as she backed her little car out of the big gates and set off toward Manton. Her meeting with Arthur Lancer was scheduled for 3.00pm and with the precious document safely tucked into her capacious handbag, she had plenty of time to take lunch with Amy and perhaps even walk the dogs along the towpath by the river before needing to keep her appointment.

As she drove through the winding lanes, she mulled over what Matilda Banner had told her. She had been a little surprised to learn of the friendship between Grace Murdock, Amy's mother, and Gran and she wondered why Amy had not mentioned it sooner. She would ask her about it when the opportunity arose. Apparently, they had regularly shared responsibility for the church flowers and other duties such as polishing the silver, cleaning the pews and mending the altar cloths. They had both, in the past, sung in the church choir and had been staunch members of the local Women's Institute; All Jam and Jerusalem, she giggled to herself. Mind you, she had to admit that she hadn't quite understood Matilda's innuendos about it being a bumpy ride at times. She had been on the point of asking for an explanation when the vicar's wife had jumped to her feet exclaiming, "Goodness, look at the time! I must be home to give Bill his lunch," and grabbing her coat had rushed out of the back door, causing a small whirlwind that had redistributed the recently rescued pile of letters which then fluttered around the kitchen in a renewed effort to lose themselves.

Bill was already sitting at the kitchen table when Matilda crashed through the back door. "Where have you been?" he opined in a disgruntled manner, "You knew I was going to be in a hurry today. I have to pay a visit to the school this afternoon to meet the new inspector..."

"I know, I know, I'm sorry," Matilda cut in and there it was again, that little niggle of doubt. It wasn't like Bill to be so critical of her, "I've already made your soup, it'll only take a minute or two to heat through. Here, perhaps you could butter the bread rolls?" She passed him the bag of fresh bread and a butter knife, hoping that activity would appease his angst. All feelings of satisfaction from her morning's pleasurable visit were gone in an instant and the recently familiar sense of discomfort, something akin to wearing an ill-fitting garment, washed over her. She sat down to eat her own serving of the homemade soup but before she had eaten more than a couple of spoonfuls, Bill, having rapidly finished his, stood up, saying, "I'll probably be late back, you know what these meetings are like..." and he was gone.

No, she didn't know what these meetings were like! To be honest, she wasn't particularly interested either, but they never used to intrude on their time together and it had been rare for Bill to be late home after such occasions. However, lateness was becoming the norm and she was beginning to think that something serious was affecting her relationship with her beloved husband. And she didn't like it, not one little bit!

Chapter 12

Copper's Corner

The small, low bungalow was almost hidden by the huge hedge that grew on three sides of the plot. Behind the property and edging a concrete yard, was the stable block. There were three stalls but these days only one was occupied by a horse. The other two housed two bicycles, an ancient motor scooter and all the associated paraphernalia for feeding the equine occupant and maintaining the wheeled transport. In one corner of the third space was a large dog cage, currently unoccupied but kept for the purpose of housing stray dogs if one should happen to materialise.

Copper's Corner, was a joke invented by the occupant's brother, intended to amuse all those who came to realise that this is where MPC Carter resided and had her headquarters. The joke was compounded by Helen Carter's gloriously red hair, strands of which often escaped from her riding helmet, leaving no doubt as to its colour and curly nature. Helen often cursed her hair but at least it made her an instantly recognisable figure as she patrolled the villages and byways of her 'patch'. It was unusual for a mounted policewoman, or man for that matter, to be appointed outside the metropolitan police force but there remained some rural areas wherein a mounted patrol was deemed more effective than a motorised unit. As a concession to modernity, Helen had been granted a bicycle and had bought the old scooter for herself. There were times when her horse was tired or the weather too inclement and, on these occasions, the wheeled transport was invaluable.

When the call had come on that unexpected occasion, she had been in the process of tacking up in readiness for her afternoon patrol of the nearby villages. Guinness, so named for his shiny black coat and frothy white mane, stood patiently while she fastened his cheek-strap and girth, checked the stirrup leathers and hoof guards before clambering onto the stone mounting block and swinging herself into the saddle. She had carried out this routine many times before and it had by now become second nature and far preferable to inserting a key into the ignition of a motorised patrol car. She tapped Guinness lightly on his rump with her short crop and squeezed her heels into his flanks. Instead of turning left out of the gate to follow her usual route via Layton and Little Winding, she turned right towards Hingemont and the churchyard to which she had been summonsed. Once on the road, she encouraged Guinness into a quick trot and arrived at the church some twenty minutes later. Twenty minutes in which many things had occurred and which would prove to make the investigation rather more complicated than it might have been had her arrival been more precipitate.

She was greeted by an incoherent and hysterical Charlie who was alternately weeping and making animal-like guttural sounds, not unlike someone choking. Charlie was well known in the local area as a cheerful if simple minded chap who helped out on Hingemont Farm and at the Manor House. He was often to be found tending graves and cutting the grass at the various local churches and could be relied on to do any of the more menial tasks involved in keeping the poorly attended places of worship in good order. Old Charlie's hands were covered in blood which was also smeared across his jacket and trousers where he had attempted to wipe away the sticky red substance. He tugged Helen's leg so hard that she slid from the saddle and landed more-or-less in his arms. Steadying her with his other arm he dragged her bodily round the church to the far side where she saw, to her dismay, the prone figure of an elderly lady who appeared to be lying in a pool of her own blood. Nearby was a blood-stained rock, large enough to have caused significant injury had it been wielded with enough force.

Realising that this situation was beyond her remit and that she would need considerable backup to deal with what she had discovered, Helen quickly pulled out her mobile phone and called the station in Manton for help. Whilst waiting for the arrival of a patrol car and, hopefully, at least two more officers and an ambulance, she set about soothing the distraught Charlie, tethered Guinness to the wrought iron post of the lych-gate and finally ascertained what she already knew; that the elderly lady was definitely dead. Although she wasn't suspicious of Charlie, protocol demanded that she caution him and handcuff him which inevitably set off a fresh spate of hysterics and it was whilst she was dealing with him that she heard the sirens wailing in the distance and breathed a sigh of relief that her burden would soon be shared.

Charlie was eventually calm enough to explain that he wanted to put away his tools. Careful as ever to do as he was expected and to look after his privileged position, he stumbled away from her, his cuffed hands outstretched and indicating a shovel that was lying, partially hidden in the long grass. Realising the significance of the blood-stained item, Helen pulled on her latex gloves and carefully pushed aside the surrounding vegetation. The implement was far too big to put in a specimen bag so she made a note in her book and a mental note to tell the officers when they arrived. She had a little trouble explaining to Charlie that he mustn't touch the shovel and definitely couldn't put it away in the shed but after a further outburst of guttural grumbling, he subsided into muttering complaints and sat down on a headstone to await further developments.

For a while she pondered who had called her. It had been so unexpected that she had only briefly registered a woman's voice, the words 'murder', 'hysterics' and 'blood' and was relying on her phone's records for further details about the caller. There would be time to investigate that once the immediate issues were dealt with.

Whilst Charlie sat rocking back and forth on the headstone, she walked carefully round the churchyard, keeping him in her sight at all times. That meant that she couldn't go to the far side of the church and so did not see the tyre tracks in the mud by the main, gated entrance to the small car park. Neither did she see the discarded purse where it lay amongst the brambles in the hedgerow but on returning to her position near Charlie's headstone, what she did see was an extraordinary procession advancing towards her. From her left approached a figure in a motorised wheelchair and from her right, a walking stick wielding lady accompanied by a small boy. As they drew nearer and turned in through the lych-gate, all three were shouting and gesticulating wildly; the two ladies appeared to be arguing vociferously, about what she had no idea, and the small boy was excitedly gabbling about witches and school teachers. However, he stopped briefly to pet Guinness, who in his bullet-proof way had simply stepped to one side to allow the newcomers to pass, but on seeing Helen, Sammy burst into angry tears saying, "You've got to do something police lady!"

Chapter 13

Manton

Arthur leant back in his ancient office chair and passed his hands over his balding head. Well, that didn't go too badly, all things considered, he thought. It was a good job Imogen had found that all important document, things should be much more straightforward now and could remove the shadow of doubt that had been hanging over him for far too long. He was about to press the intercom and ask Amy to bring him a fresh cup of coffee when he realised that she would have left by now, it being nearly two in the afternoon. It was quite inconvenient only having her here for half of each day; he would have to speak to her about increasing her hours. The thought of spending a little more time in her company put a smile on his face and he whistled cheerfully as he walked through to the tiny office kitchenette and switched on the kettle.

Whilst he waited for the water to boil, he rummaged in the cupboard for a mug and finding a packet of biscuits, he munched hungrily on a couple of custard creams, realising that he had missed lunch entirely. He had been extremely anxious about the impending arrival of Inspector Peterson since he well remembered the last uncomfortable interview with that somewhat inflexible man. He had the ability to make even the most innocent of people feel guilty and the resulting tongue tied, incoherent, garbled nonsense that one was inclined to utter only added to the impression of culpability. You would have thought that a man of the law, like himself, would be immune from such effects, but no, even Percival Arthur Lancer was reduced to a gibbering wreck in the presence of Patrick Peterson.

Arthur remembered all too clearly his embarrassment at the accusations thrown at him by old Mrs Springfield shortly after the demise of her husband. He had tried very hard to be charitable and to understand that she was distraught and probably not thinking very clearly, but despite his efforts she had managed to undermine his confidence and reduced him almost to tears with her uncharacteristic vitriol and vehemence. It had all been to do with Mr Springfield's eccentric Will.

It had eventually been sorted out a long time ago; well it must have been several years at least since Mr Springfield had passed away. The case had gone to Court and Mrs Springfield had won her appeal which had put Arthur in an awkward financial situation since she had also been awarded costs meaning that not only was he responsible for the court fees but neither had he been paid for his time and trouble in attempting to uphold the Will held by his company. Unfortunately, the consequent poverty, as a result of the necessity of a bank loan, had contributed to his wife's departure, which also proved to be an expensive exercise and the combined circumstances had led to his return to his mother's abode. Not an ideal arrangement but one which had its advantages and which was certainly beneficial from a monetary point of view. He was grateful that his mother had avoided the smug and tempting "I told you she was trouble. I've known her for a long time now... always upsetting the apple-cart that one!"

He really didn't understand how anyone could suspect him of holding a grudge; it just wasn't in his nature. Nevertheless, Inspector Peterson had made all sorts of unpleasant suggestions and accusations about how he wanted to get revenge and how his wife's leaving him had turned his mind. Apparently, "We've had one or two complaints made against you sir," claimed Peterson, "You'd be surprised how many people think that you're on the take with your lawyer's fees and commissions." He was bluffing of course; he had to be didn't he? The business was doing reasonably well and his fees were no higher than any other Solicitor's office. In any case they were advised by the Legal Society guidelines and, if anything, he always charged the minimum possible unless he was certain that a client could well afford to pay more. Arthur had been stung by the remarks, but his lawyer status had provided him with a comparatively thick skin and he stuck to his insistence that there had been no wrong doing with regard to Ada Springfield's affairs.

"Well, I don't know what you'd call it, but I'd say that murder is wrongdoing of the highest order!" retorted Inspector Peterson. Murder? Had she been murdered? Was he being accused of murder? Surely not? The awful prospect of being charged with a murder he had not committed, hung over poor Arthur for almost a week. On that first day, following several hours incarcerated in the cold, stark and miserable interview room at Manton Police Station, he had been released with a caution and with instructions to not leave town which was not a problem since he had no intention of going anywhere until this ridiculous situation was resolved.

Thank goodness today's visit had ruled out any suggestion of his needing to take revenge or any other motive for violence against the old lady. Truth to tell he had rather liked Ada and had great respect for her insistence that her dear husband, had he been of sound mind at the time he wrote that last ridiculous will, would never have left his entire estate to the Church and his flock of Jacob's sheep. Arthur had only felt obliged to defend the will on the grounds of it having been drawn up in his office by his former employer and on the basis of it undermining his veracity had it proven to be invalid. As it was and as we have already discovered, his reputation and his pocket had taken a significant blow when he lost the case, but he had made his peace with Ada and had been entrusted by her to draw up her current will; the one which Imogen had eventually discovered and presented to him yesterday. Not only did it demonstrate a sound working relationship between the two but it also negated any suspicion of lingering retribution regarding the former misunderstanding.

Today's meeting with Inspector Peterson had ruled out any prospect of his being charged with wrongdoing concerning the current situation. Indeed Peterson had almost apologised when he took his leave, "I hope I haven't caused you too much inconvenience but you'll appreciate the necessity of examining every aspect," and he left, without a proffered hand for a gentlemanly shake but with a brief, courteous nod of the head in Arthur's general direction.

Coffee drunk and the day's business concluded, Arthur decided to lock up the office a little early and take a slow drive home. Perhaps he would go via Hingemont and see for himself where the unfortunate occurrence had taken place. He had just picked up his keys and shrugged his overcoat onto his shoulders when the phone began to ring. He hesitated for a moment or two before reluctantly picking up the receiver...

Chapter 14

Layton Farm

The last thing Farmer Franklin wanted was trouble. It was difficult enough to balance the demands of the land, the crops, the finances and the workers without there being unexpected interruptions beyond the inevitable ones that nature threw at him. It was then, with considerable irritation, that he had watched the blue lights drawing nearer and nearer to his property. There being no other dwellings nearby and since his office and farmhouse were set well back from the road at the end of a track that was almost a mile long, there could be no doubt that his was the intended destination for the unmistakable vehicle which approached.

On that particular afternoon, he had already been inconvenienced by a shortage of workers. Thierry had come to him shortly after breakfast to inform him that several of the recently arrived workforces were complaining of headaches and stomach cramps and were therefore deemed unable to work at harvesting the produce. It wouldn't do for them to contaminate the crop with whatever particular virus they were all harbouring. Their sickness meant there would be serious risk of delay in getting the produce ready for shipping off to market the following day and a knock-on effect if things weren't sorted out quickly. Franklin had been obliged to call his neighbouring farmer to enquire as to whether they had any men to spare. Fortunately, Mr Meakin was able to provide a handful of willing workers, mainly women, who would come to help.

"Thank goodness," Franklin had breathed in semi relief, "not exactly ideal, but certainly better than losing a whole day!" he sighed to no one in particular. Little did he know that his troubles had only just begun.

Franklin was not a hard man. He loved the land and he loved his work, but he found people very trying. An insular being, he preferred to keep his distance from the hired men; not because he didn't like them but simply because he didn't really know how to interact with them and, of course, there was always the language barrier. For as long as Franklin could remember, and certainly throughout his father's time, foreign workers had always been shipped in to help with the harvest. In the early days most of the men came from Poland but nowadays they came from many of the Eastern European countries and the latest contingent had arrived from Lithuania just a few days prior to the particular afternoon in question.

On the day in question, was it really only last Friday, Thierry had hurried across the farmyard to stand beside Franklin as the police car drew into the yard. Two burly officers stepped out of the vehicle and greeted the waiting men, not unkindly but in a very business-like manner.

"It seems we have a bit of a problem with one of your employees," began the more senior of the two. "Says his name is Otto Vaso... something and he works here." Thierry peered in through the car window and nodded to Franklin, affirming the identity of the man in the back seat, "had an idea he was going to be trouble," he muttered.

"Ah!" grunted Franklin, "what seems to be the matter?"

"Well to start with he doesn't seem to speak much English and to continue, he doesn't have a driving license."

"Nor a vehicle!" exclaimed Thierry in surprise.

"That's as maybe," retorted the second officer, "but it didn't seem to stop him from driving at dangerously high speed down some narrow lanes in someone else's car!"

"Kas vyksta?" asked Otto Vasovich as he clambered awkwardly, hands cuffed behind him, out of the back of the police car.

"Oi! Where do you think you're going?" demanded the first officer, PC Johns, "get back in there at once!"

"Nesuprantu," Otto looked pleadingly at Thierry who didn't understand Lithuanian either, "Je ne comprends pas," he replied loudly, in his native French in vain hope that the man might understand that better.

"Well here's a pretty state of affairs," said Franklin, "it seems that we need an interpreter or two, but I think it might be helpful if you could explain a little about what has happened?"

"All in good time," said Johns. "First things first though. Get that man back in the car," he said to his companion, "then I think we need to get down to the station to make sure everything is official. Can you follow us down there sir? And bring someone who speaks the lingo?"

It was only later that Franklin wondered how the police officers knew where to bring Otto given his diminutive grasp of the English language but it seemed that Otto could repeat the names 'Franklin' and 'Layton' and the officers, no doubt using some of their detective skill, had put two and two together and been able to make an accurate, educated guess.

Much later, after a lengthy and protracted interview at Manton Police headquarters, Franklin, Thierry and an exhausted interpreter returned to Layton Farm. Otto was to be held overnight at the station since there were many unexplained circumstances, not least of which was his potential involvement in the death of an elderly lady who had been found in Hingemont Churchyard in close proximity to where Otto claimed to have 'found' the car he 'borrowed'. At the suggestion of his involvement in wrong doing of such magnitude, he had cried out in alarm, "Ne! Aš nieko nenužudžiau!" and had become increasingly agitated; even tending towards violence. It was at that point that the decision had been made to hold Otto overnight pending finding him a suitable lawyer and further enquiries into both the theft of the car, resulting in the dangerous driving, and the dead lady. A stream of incomprehensible Lithuanian protests, which even the longsuffering interpreter found unintelligible, resulted in the distraught foreigner being frogmarched away by two further officers who were obviously not going to stand for any nonsense.

No one observed the distress etched on poor Otto's face as he, throughout a very long night, unable to sleep, contemplated his likely future in this bleak place. If only he had not succumbed to the temptation of a joy-ride in that oh so tempting vehicle and the readily available keys, just lying there on the grass... Of course, he should not have taken the money from that purse and he was quite prepared to accept any retribution for having done so, but murder? How could they think that of him, Otto Vasovich, son of Maria and fiancée to his beloved Natalya, and only here to try to make a little money for their future? And now? What would become of him? What would become of them? It just didn't bear thinking about and Otto Vasovich, wept.

And so, it was that much later that evening, Farmer Franklin sank into his comfy armchair with a soothing glass of whisky and a troubled mind. He really didn't want any trouble but a potential murderer amongst his workers was definitely trouble with a capital T.

Chapter 15

Partington Hall

'Arthur had sounded really rather disgruntled,' Amy mused to herself. She too felt a little put out by his response to her call; especially since she had battled with herself for some considerable time before eventually picking up her phone and dialling the office number. She wasn't at all sure that inviting Arthur's mother to tea with Grace was a good idea, particularly bearing in mind their historic enmity. The two ladies were renowned for their loud and vociferous arguments, usually about nothing important, and the names Grace and Mary had become synonymous with upset in the small village community. Mind you, truth to tell, the names of Ada and Grace were not much better and over the years it had become increasingly clear that the main culprit was Grace herself. There was nothing she liked more than a good quarrel!

It was her uncertainty that had resulted in a phone call to Arthur, rather than the more direct approach of waiting until she was at work the following day. It was also at the insistence of her mother that she, "get to it girl! What are you waiting for?" Once Grace had an idea in her head, there was no putting it off. Amy tried so hard to be sympathetic of her mother's disability but it was actually quite amazing to see just what exactly she could achieve when she set her mind to something.

One example of Grace's determination had been the installation of the cumbersome stair lift which, as already described, caused Amy not inconsiderable inconvenience when ascending to the first-floor bedroom where Grace spent most of her time. The second demand that Grace had made was the acquisition of a motorised wheelchair – well more of a mobility scooter, equipped with all mod cons such as a rain cover and larger wheels to cope with the uneven village roads and pathways. This had also been a mixed blessing since Grace was not very expert in manoeuvring the thing and had several times needed rescuing from an awkward situation. It amazed Amy that Grace managed to get anywhere at all and she often found herself wondering just how disadvantaged her mother really was.

Quickly, she dismissed the uncharitable thought. Of course she had witnessed her mother's suffering and hadn't she been delighted that her mother was regaining a little of her former independence? She drank the last of her, now cold, tea and pulled on her wellingtons. She really should go and clean the muddy wheels of the aforementioned vehicle and plug the battery in to charge in readiness for her mother's next foray into the great outdoors.

Pip uncurled his little body from in front of the stove and, wagging furiously, he bounced round her legs as she shrugged into her overcoat and went out into the yard and to the stable come garage where the scooter was stored. She filled a bucket at the outdoor tap and took a scrubbing brush from the shelf. It shouldn't take long and she would get it gleaming, just as her mother liked it, leaving plenty of time to cook the evening meal. Perhaps she could even bake a cake in readiness for Mary Lancer's visit tomorrow afternoon.

It was as she took a cloth to polish the front mudguard that she noticed the discoloration. Everywhere else she had polished the shiny white bodywork until it shone, except for this last part over the front wheel. Here there were streaks of orange or rust; not the brown mud that had easily washed away. Amy peered more closely and scratched at one of the smears which came off onto her fingernail. Puzzled, she sniffed at the residue and smelt a metallic aroma which was both familiar and unusual. Something warned Amy that this was not quite right and she hesitated before scrubbing harder in an attempt to remove the stains. She didn't want to damage the surface of the paintwork but somehow, she felt it was important to leave no trace of whatever this substance was.

A little later, Amy made her way back into the warm kitchen. She ran her hands under the hot tap, groaning a little as the water brought her cold fingers back to life. As the feeling returned, the scent of the substance she had washed away was suddenly stronger and immediately she recognised it as blood. Blood? Oh my goodness! How on earth could blood have got on there? Had Grace hit something? A cat, a rabbit, a dog or... even a child? Amy's hand flew to her mouth at the thought. Surely she would have mentioned having done such a thing? She may be sour old woman, but she loved animals and she certainly wasn't cruel. She would have been very upset had she caused injury to some innocent creature. Amy determined to address· the question later when her mother was awake for supper but as it happens events took an unexpected turn and the opportunity was lost.

Amy's thoughts were interrupted by an insistent knocking on the front door... She was astonished to see Arthur standing on her doorstep. After her initial dumbstruck reaction, she quickly regained her composure and invited him in. He, awkwardly, removed his hat and coat, dumping them on a chair as he passed it in the hallway and followed her into the parlour which was chilly due to disuse.

"You'll be wondering..."

"What, I mean why, I mean..." they both spoke at once and then laughed uncomfortably. A short silence ensued and then, "How can I help?" asked Amy.

Arthur explained that he thought it best to come in person because he didn't quite know how to interpret his mother's extreme reaction to Amy's invitation to tea the following day and he didn't want to appear rude or dismissive by a rather impersonal telephone call.

"She threw an absolutely hysterical fit when I told her you'd invited her!" he said, "I've never seen her so upset and I must admit that it frightened me somewhat. I thought she might have a heart attack or something."

"Did she explain why?" asked Amy, "I mean, why it was so upsetting to be invited here for tea?"

"I don't think it was anything to do with you," Arthur quickly reassured the girl, "it was to do with your mother. She was screaming about never wanting to see her again, about how she is a wicked, awful and evil woman..." he stopped abruptly, "Oh I'm really sorry – how rude of me, talking about your mother like that..."

Amy laughed at his embarrassment, "Don't worry," she said, "I'm well aware of my mother's shortcomings. She means well but her manner can leave an awful lot to be desired!"

Sometime later, after a comforting cup of tea and a mutually satisfying chat, Arthur left with a slight spring in his step, a smile on his face, and the determination that his and Amy's mother should meet no matter the consequences. He would bring her to tea tomorrow whether she like it or not!

Accordingly, at three in the afternoon the following day, Amy opened the door to a smiling Arthur and a very sour faced Mary Lancer. She had obviously been berating her son for tricking her into doing that which she had said she would not and in order to prevent her from leaving, he had her arm very securely tucked into his elbow. Despite her ire, it was clear to Amy that there was more to her distress than simple irritation. Behind the angry glaze to her eyes was fear and Amy wondered of what exactly Mary Lancer could be afraid.

She led the visitors into the front sitting room where a log fire blazed in the hearth, warming the room. The weak sunshine peeked in through the big bay window and highlighted the diminutive figure seated in a big armchair and with a tartan rug wrapped around her legs and lap. Grace looked up at the newcomers and held out a sparrow like hand, "Welcome," she said.

It was a total surprise to them all when Mary Lancer, abruptly, inexplicably and without any warning, burst into tears.

Chapter 16

Hingemont House – Ada

Ada Springfield liked to keep busy. She was determined to be active as long as she possibly could. Her house and garden were her pride and joy and had been her home for nearly sixty years. She was not a busybody or a gossip but she kept her eye on the village community and knew most of what was going on; even that which ostensibly took place behind closed doors. She was involved with the Church, the School and the Village Hall activities including the WI, the Girl Guides and the Scouting movement. She was well loved by all and had only ever quarrelled with Grace Murdock, although there was nothing particularly unusual in that – everyone had fallen out with Grace at one time or another.

On the back of her cloakroom door was a small poster, given to her by her beloved granddaughter, Imogen, its legend stated, "Don't stop doing things because you are getting old because you will only get old when you stop doing things." It was the mantra by which she lived in her declining years and especially since her husband had died. She liked to think of herself as, not exactly a merry widow, but certainly a positive widow with a passion for life that was undiminished by her years and her circumstances. Obviously, there were things that were much more difficult to accomplish as age took its toll, but she continued to tend her garden, keep her own house clean and tidy and help out wherever she could in the small village community.

To this end she undertook responsibility for the Church flower arranging. Not just to do it herself but to organise a rota of flower providers and arrangers. Since she lived very near to the church, she nearly always attended on 'flower day' to ensure that whoever's turn it was had arrived on time and knew what to do and where everything was stored. Invariably this included unlocking the Church to allow ingress to the designated party. The only exceptions to this practise were Grace Murdock and Mary Lancer who were both fully versed in the process and in the whereabouts of the required key. It wasn't exactly a secret but it wasn't general knowledge either and only a handful of people, including the venerable ladies, knew of the hiding place. However, there was one other, somewhat unlikely person, who had the information – little Sammy Jenkins.

On the afternoon of a series of unfortunate events, Ada made her way haltingly down the gravelled driveway of Hingemont House, through the gate, carefully closed behind her, left through the village and past the very small community Hall. She rarely, if ever, saw anyone on this regular commute and as she turned left towards the church, had been surprised on that occasion to see Mary Lancer's small car parked outside The Manse which was located just beyond the church itself. As she drew nearer to the lychgate she saw Mary step out of the front door of the Manse and wave a cheery goodbye to Matilda who, with her apron fluttering in the gentle breeze, waved in return.

They met as they both reached the gate at the same moment and both turned their heads to see from whence an unexpected sound was emanating. A high-pitched whirring, not unlike an electric lawn mower accompanied the strange sight of an elderly figure hunched over the handlebars of a mobility scooter. Of course, there is nothing strange about an elderly person on a mobility scooter but this particular person had on her face the fiercest expression imaginable and was gripping the handlebars as if her very life depended on her not letting go. Besides this, there was a strange assortment of objects hanging from her being and some rather precariously balance bags which would have been more appropriately affixed to the saddle on a horse. On her head was an ancient riding hat and in her hand was the sort of whip that might have been used to spur and control a wayward steed.

"Oh my…"

"Whatever next…" Ada and Mary spoke in unison just as Grace Murdock yelled a cheery, "What ho you two!" A quick exchange of raised eyebrows and a wry grin before the first two ladies greeted the newcomer with somewhat false enthusiasm.

"How lovely to see you out and about," remarked Mary and, "Wherever did you find such an – erm – interesting vehicle?" enquired Ada.

Grace explained, not exactly truthfully, that Amy had suggested the scooter along with the stair-lift that enabled her to get downstairs unaided. You would have thought that she might have been grateful for her new found freedom of sorts but it seems that not even this was enough to persuade her to be pleased to be able to meet her friends without relying on someone else to transport her to and fro. The habitual scowl rarely left her brow and her whole demeanour was one of dissatisfaction with life, people and just about everything. It did occur to Mary to wonder why on earth Grace would want to come down to the church to help when all she did was to find fault with whatever anyone else was attempting to do. Ada on the other hand was more magnanimous in her approach and in her usual benevolent manner suggested things that she thought Grace would be able to achieve from her seated position on the scooter.

Thus it was that when the first obstacle to their mission; the missing key, was discovered, Grace was dispatched to the Manse to enquire whether either the Rev. Bill or his wife knew of its whereabouts. Mary volunteered to make her way to the village store which was only five-minute's walk away, she 'could do with the exercise', she declared as she patted her rounded stomach and set off briskly on foot, and Ada began a more thorough search of the churchyard.

From his vantage point halfway up the old Yew Tree that stood in the corner of the churchyard, Sammy Jenkins sniggered to himself as he listened to the three old ladies bickering vociferously as to whose fault it was that the key was mislaid. First one said it couldn't have been put back properly last time, then another said that she hadn't been the last to use it, and the third declared that she always put it back where it lived and they were all talking very loudly and all at the same time so that none of them noticed as he slipped down from his lookout and made his way over the wall and into the field that ran behind the village school and Miss Lester's cottage. There was something else that had captured his interest and he wanted to confirm his suspicion...

Once the first two ladies had been dispatched on their errands, Ada began to continue searching the churchyard and surrounding area. Surely the key couldn't be far away? The container was quite distinctive and, in any case, why would anyone wish to remove it? Had someone used the key to enter the church, there might have been sense in its removal, but there were no signs of anyone having opened the big old door and until she managed to get inside, she couldn't possibly tell whether anything had been disturbed. Certainly, the donations of flowers that had been placed in the buckets of water provided for that purpose, were still in front of the door in the porch and it seemed unlikely that anyone else had been inside since they would definitely have had to have moved the buckets in order to open the door.

She could hear Old Charlie whistling to himself as he mowed the grass on the far side of the church. She noticed that the storage shed door was ajar and she could see the assortment of tools, jam jars and vases provided for flowers on graves, the shovels for digging and the rake for smoothing the disturbed earth on a newly filled in grave. She noticed the paint tins, the hammers and jars of nails and the other prerequisites for maintaining the grounds and the interior of the old church. As she was walking carefully along the perimeter of the church walls, searching in the longer grass for the missing item, she failed to notice that which was her eventual undoing. All that she did observe was a very loud noise, a sudden blow to her head which was followed by complete silence, blackness and nothing more.

Chapter 17

Sammy

He wasn't at all sure what he was seeing. He was somewhat precariously balanced on top of the rickety bicycle shelter in the corner of the school playground. From this dubious vantage point he could just about see into Miss Lester's bedroom but the window was very small, the curtains billowing in the breeze and because the window was open, a little the sunlight caused reflections which further obscured his view. He could however hear some very unusual noises. At first, he had thought that someone was ill; there were sighs and moans, but then he heard what sounded like giggles and laughter. He really couldn't be sure. He was very surprised when he realised that the Reverend was in Miss Lester's room and that he seemed to be wrestling with someone – maybe even Miss Lester herself? The noises quietened a bit and he was on the point of clambering down from his risky position when he was startled by a loud scream and a guttural groan. He really didn't know what to make of it and truth to tell he was a bit disturbed. He might ask his mum, if she wasn't too busy, but then he'd have to admit that he had been spying – perhaps that wasn't such a good idea after all. He'd have to bide his time…

Sammy decided to make his way back to the churchyard. He wanted to know whether they had found the key yet and it was funny watching the old ladies arguing and getting so cross with each other!

It was as he noticed the lady on the scooter that it occurred to him. Dressed all in black with her peculiar headgear and sitting astride the bag festooned vehicle she looked just like a witch on a broomstick. "That's it!" he exclaimed to himself, "I knew it all the time!" and he ran wildly toward the other lady, the one with a walking stick. "You have to do something..." he yelled to the astonished Mary, just as she noticed MPC Pepper dismounting from Guinness and hooking his reins over the lych-gate post.

Grace had never driven her scooter so fast. She had heard the yelling of Sammy and hurried to see what was going on. Mary was shouting at the irate boy, Grace was shouting to Mary and Sammy was gabbling about goodness knows what. Helen Carter apprehended all three of them and insisted that they stay just inside the gate and under no circumstances were they to go round to the other side of the church. It was all extremely puzzling and when the sirens were first heard and then seen approaching at speed, Mary sat down heavily on a conveniently placed bench and Sammy burst into tears.

The noisy arrival of the police and ambulance inevitably drew a small crowd of inquisitive onlookers. At first Helen was occupied in insisting that they kept their distance and didn't disturb anything that might be significant to any ensuing investigation and at the same time was careful not to reveal the nature of the emergency. Once the intrusive villagers had been persuaded to go away, she turned her attention to the two elderly ladies. A couple of quick phone calls and Amy and Arthur were soon on their way to rescue their respective mothers. It was entirely coincidental at this point that both Amy and Arthur were involved since this all took place before they had officially met and at the time there had been no suggestion of any future connection. In fact, due to the separate and differing distances involved they did not meet on this occasion. Amy arrived first and was ably assisted by a burly policeman who bundled Grace into the front seat of his car and drove the two of them the short distance to Partington Hall with a promise to deliver the scooter home as soon as convenient once the immediate issues had been dealt with.

Arthur arrived just as Grace and Amy's transport disappeared around a corner. He found a distraught and bewildered Mary still slumped on the bench and muttering about her friends, what had happened and if only she hadn't taken so long to walk to the shop. It took Arthur a long time to get to the bottom of the story and it was several days later, after the entrance of Amy, via the agency, into his employ, when he had decided that Mary and Grace should meet to talk about the events of that extraordinary afternoon. Both ladies had been extremely disturbed by the occurrences and he thought it would help them both to talk about it. Concurrently, Amy had come to the same conclusion and once they had both realised the connection between his mother's arch enemy and Amy's mother, Arthur had been more than pleased to accept the invitation to tea.

~

Once the two ladies had been dispatched to their individual homes, Helen looked at the tear stained and angry faced Sammy. She wondered what on earth could have distressed him to such an extent. She was quite certain that he hadn't witnessed Ada's accident and as far as she could tell he was completely unaware of what had happened. All he could talk about was witches and devils and exterminating demons and he was obviously very upset, especially because no one appeared to be taking him seriously and they were all preoccupied with something which meant nothing at all to him.

Eventually, she took him to his home. He was met by an impatient mother, a disinterested father and a granny who folded him into her arms, patted his head and murmured, "There, there dear – I told you, you shouldn't poke your nose into things that don't concern you." Having assured herself that he was at least safe for the time being, she made a note to request social services to check his situation and took her leave. She would be pleased to get home, rub Guinness down and turn him out for the evening, and to sit down with a welcome cup of tea.

Chapter 18

Partington Hall

A fresh pot of tea, a box of tissues, a comfortable chair and the warmth of the fire soon soothed the distraught tears and Mary, sniffing occasionally and with a grateful, though watery smile at Amy, muttered her apologies for having made a scene. Grace snorted ungraciously and was about to make some derogatory remark when Amy spoke loudly, "Please don't be sorry, the whole situation has been most distressing and the reason for asking you to come here is to try to get to the bottom of the puzzling circumstances." She paused before continuing, "and I really think it might be time that you and my mother bury the hatchet. Don't you agree Mother?" she enquired pointedly of her mother's averted face. She was a little surprised to notice that her mother wiped a tear from her own eye as she turned to face the other three occupants of the room.

Arthur shuffled uncomfortably in the presence of the two tearful women and wondered how soon he could make his escape. He looked across at Amy and was amused to see her grimacing at him as it became apparent that she too was discomforted. "Perhaps you could begin by explaining what you were all doing at the church last week?" she suggested.

Mary began, "We had arranged to meet up to sort out the flowers for Sunday. People are very kind with donating blooms from their gardens and all we need to do is to change the alter cloth, arrange the flowers and make sure all is neat, tidy and polished for the service. In order to do this, we need to get into the building and there is a key that is kept hidden for that purpose. We all know where it is but this time it wasn't there."

"Somebody had removed it!" Grace interrupted accusingly.

"Yes, it wasn't there…"

"You mean no it wasn't there!"

"No, I mean yes it wasn't there…"

"So, what happened next?" Arthur diverted the pending quarrel with the skill of a barrister.

"I was told to go and ask at The Manse," Grace emphasised the word 'told' as if it had been a military command, "So I went there. The Reverend was elsewhere and his dear wife, Matilda seemed a bit distracted, but she invited me in and had a quick look on the hook where the key is normally kept. It wasn't there and when she saw that I was troubled she offered me a cup of tea which she had just prepared. I accepted it. It's quite hard work steering that new-fangled machine you bought me." She looked pointedly at Amy before continuing, "anyway we chatted a bit and then I said I needed to report back to Ada and hope that a key had been found elsewhere. So, I left." She drew breath to continue but Mary took the opportunity to butt in, "I was dispatched to the village shop where we know they keep an emergency key." She began, eager to give her version of events now that Grace had told her part.

"It's quite a walk to that shop for legs as old as mine and when I arrived, there were several people waiting ahead of me. I took the opportunity to rest on the wall outside for a minute or two and when I did eventually ask Deidre she reminded me that the key had been borrowed a few weeks ago and hadn't been returned yet. So, I too drew a blank and made my way back to the church to tell the others."

"It was quite a shock…"

"Imagine how upsetting it was…" both ladies began to speak at once and Arthur held up his hand, "One at a time please!" he demanded, "Mrs Murdock, you first."

"I saw Helen Carter dismounting from her horse and wondered what on earth she was doing there. I suppose I'd been gone for about twenty minutes and it would have taken her nearly that long to get there assuming she was coming from her home. Of course, she might have been somewhere nearer than that but I wouldn't know. When we got close enough, she stopped us and told us that we mustn't go round to the other side of the church. I was quite annoyed because I wanted to tell Ada about the key! I told her so but she insisted that we should stay where we were."

"Yes!" Mary joined in, "It was very upsetting to be prevented from doing what we needed to do. At our age, its' all too easy to forget a message unless we can repeat it fairly immediately."

"Speak for yourself!" retorted Grace.

Mary glared at her before continuing. "And there was that very irritating little Sammy who was making me feel quite dizzy as he jumped all over the place yelling about witches and demons and ex, ex, exor somethings."

"Exorcisms," Grace corrected drily, "that's what he meant but he didn't say it quite right. I've no idea what he was really trying to get at but it was something to do with Miss Lester. I never did like that one…"

"You never like anyone…" interjected Mary.

"Now, now, no need to start all that again," said Amy. "I suppose you both do know what had happened by now?"

"Yes, poor Ada," said Mary, "We know what happened but we don't know how or why. Who would do such an awful thing to a lovely person like Ada Springfield? And that poor granddaughter of hers, Imogen isn't it?" She didn't wait for an answer but suddenly put her hand to her mouth, "Oh!" she exclaimed, "I've just had a terrible thought! What has happened to my car?"

"Your car?" questioned Arthur, "Isn't it in the garage at home?"

"No!" Mary's eyes were as big as saucers, "I've just remembered, I drove to the church last week and you took me home Arthur! But my car isn't where I left it! I haven't even thought about it until now – I've been that upset. I know I parked it near the church but I didn't take it to the shop, I walked there."

"I expect you forgot that too," remarked Grace with a snide grin and Mary looked as though she might lash out at her but instead retorted, "No! I did not!"

"But you did forget about it until now!" Grace was enjoying her superiority but before she could make more of her friend's failing memory, Arthur commented, "Well, I suppose we must report it missing. I'll phone the police straight away," and he left the room pulling his mobile phone from his pocket as he did so.

"More tea anyone?" offered Amy in a conciliatory tone and without waiting for an answer, she took the pot to refresh it in the kitchen.

Grace and Mary sat in silence for a minute or two until Grace rummaged in her pocket and pulled out a slightly crumpled and faded photograph. She handed it wordlessly to Mary who took it, squinted at it with a puzzled expression and after a minute or two, gasped, laughed and burst into tears again.

"There's no need to cry," said Grace gruffly, "I don't mean to upset you. I just thought perhaps we should remember a happier time if we're supposed to be making up. I asked Amy to find my old photograph albums a few days ago and on looking through them I came across this one and a few others like it. Do you remember those days? We were free, happy and an inseparable threesome that summer. I must admit it quite upset me when I was reminded of how things were back then. Look at us! What happened? When did we become so distant and so angry with each other? I can only assume it was a man or men or a difference of opinion over something trivial." She paused and dabbed at her eye in an uncharacteristic display of emotion, "Anyway, I want to say I'm sorry. It doesn't come easy to me to apologise but losing Ada has been a big blow and..." she hiccoughed quietly, "and I don't want to lose you as well. Can we bury the hatchet and be friends again?"

When first Arthur and then Amy returned to the room, one bearing news and the other a fresh pot of tea, they were astonished to find the two ladies sitting side by side with their heads bent over an album and laughing quietly together.

Chapter 19

Hingemont House

The loud knocking at the big old front door woke Imogen from her reverie. Benjy barked too and the unexpected noise alarmed her. She scrambled to her feet, dropping the unread book as she did so, tripped over the forgotten rug draped over her knees and hurried to the door.

Her delight in seeing her brother, Max, on the doorstep was only tempered by her curiosity as to why he had come unannounced, and on a work day. She had hoped that he and Archie might arrive at the weekend but this was only Thursday.

"Well aren't you going to invite me in?" Max grinned at his sister and held out his arms at the ends of which his hands held large carrier bags overflowing with provisions and other goodies. Imogen flew at him and almost bowled him over. She wrapped her arms around his well-toned waist and hugged him tightly. "I'm so pleased to see you," she cried.

"Okay, okay," he soothed, "let me put these things down and then I can hug you properly!"

A short while later, the groceries put away and coffee drunk, Max explained that he felt it was unfair to leave Imogen to deal with the legalities and other business to do with Gran's demise, especially now that there seemed to be foul play to consider. Catherine had insisted on sending food and other domestic requirements and Max had come prepared to stay for as long as necessary.

"First things first," he said, "I really don't understand why you haven't been visited by the cops? What's all this about you having to find everything out via a lawyer? I really think we need to start asking a few very serious questions!"

Imogen breathed a sigh of relief; at last she would have someone to help her find answers to the questions that had been troubling her but which she hadn't felt confident enough to raise.

It had already been arranged for Imogen to visit the Funeral parlour the following day and she was now rather relieved that Max would go with her. She'd never seen a dead person before and was understandably a little nervous as to how she would feel. Having Max with her would be such a comfort.

Immediately after breakfast on Friday morning, Max rang Manton Police Station and after a brief conversation with a distant, disembodied voice and a stern, persuasive tone from Max making it quite clear that no was not an acceptable answer, an appointment was made for straight after the two of them had been to the mortuary.

The morning was spent sorting through various documents and important looking letters that Imogen and Matilda had unearthed when trying to make some semblance of order in Grandpa's neglected study. Most of the papers were deemed unimportant but one or two bank statements and share certificates were put aside by Max who said he was happy to investigate the financial side of things since that was his area of expertise. Imogen was more than happy to delegate that responsibility to her able brother. She was more interested in the personal letters and collectibles with which Grandpa had filled the shelves and drawers. She had no idea whether any of the various items had any real value, but she would enjoy doing some research and perhaps taking the more obscure items to an antique dealer for assessment at a later date. For now, they simply arranged things into three piles; rubbish, research and relevant.

Soon it was time to set off to Manton. Benjy was most indignant at being shut in the kitchen but the promise of a walk on her return seemed to settle him down and the Bonio biscuit distracted him long enough for her to escape without his pitiful whining tearing at her heartstrings! The luxury of being driven in Max's rather smart car allowed Imogen to relax and muse on her Gran's death. How would she look? How would Imogen react? Would it be scary or uncomfortable? They said she had a blow to the head so would there be an injury visible or maybe some bruising? Suddenly Imogen realised she was crying. She hadn't cried for Gran since arriving here – there just hadn't been time and somehow the business of dealing with the situation had over-ridden her emotions.

Max pulled the car into the Funeral Director's car park. Wordlessly he handed Imogen a tissue from a box secreted in the glove compartment, and he laid a conciliatory arm across her shoulder, "Don't be upset old thing," he soothed, "at least it was pretty quick and I'm sure she didn't suffer. Many old people have to go through months if not years of age-related agonies before they die – at least she was spared any of that." He paused while Imogen sniffed and nodded.

"I know," she mumbled into the tissue.

"Come on, pull yourself together, you've been so strong and Gran would have been very proud of you. Don't let her down now." Trust Max to be so practical but his words helped and Imogen took a deep breath and smiled a watery grin up at him. "Thanks," she said.

It was nothing like she had expected – although to be honest she hadn't really known what to expect. The room was rather cool and she pulled her cardigan closer around her shoulders as soft music played quietly. The scent of the flowers arranged decorously on either side of the ornate coffin, filled the small room. Gran didn't look like Gran at all. Gone were the crinkles at the corners of her smiling eyes, her hair was neatly swept into her habitual pleat but there were no wisps escaping and framing her rounded face. Her skin looked waxy and her mouth was held in an unnatural shape. There was nothing horrible about it at all but the overall effect was one of… well of nothing! Imogen didn't know what she felt, she didn't know what to say or think. She just stood by the coffin and stared;

her mind blank. She felt Max's hand under her elbow and heard him say, "You okay? Shall we go?" and realised that he too was perplexed. Unable to respond, she nodded and turned to leave. At the last moment she turned back, "Gran? I'm sorry," she said, "I love you..." and, "Me too," came gruffly from Max.

After a brief conversation with the funeral director and an agreement to discuss a suitable date for either cremation or interment once the police enquiries were completed, the brother and sister were pleased to leave clutching a handful of brochures for coffins, flowers and other suggestions, and to set off once more in the relative comfort of Max's car. Imogen laid her head back against the leather headrest and closed her eyes. What next? She wondered as Max drove skilfully and smoothly towards the Police headquarters in Manton town centre.

What next was actually a rather long wait. Inspector Peterson was obviously in no hurry to greet his appointees and took his time with a prolonged phone call and a discussion with another officer during which a third officer popped his head round the door of the interview room in which they waited and offered them tea or coffee. By the time Patrick Peterson eventually strode into the room both Max and Imogen were distinctly uncomfortable and more than a little frustrated at the extended delay.

Before either of them could greet the newcomer, Peterson sat down abruptly on the chair placed at the other side of a metal table which stood in the middle of the otherwise empty room. Max withdrew his proffered hand and waited.

"Sorry to have kept you waiting," Peterson began brusquely, "We seem to be very busy right now and things have been made more difficult by a series of mishaps within our ranks which have resulted in our not being able to process things as quickly as we would wish." Neither Imogen nor her brother made any response and so Peterson continued, "I'm afraid there isn't very much that I can tell you right now but feel free to ask and I'll answer if I'm able."

"Well," began Max, "first of all we'd like to know why all the information we've received so far has come via Gran's, I mean Mrs Springfield's lawyer."

"Yes, I realise that's a bit unusual but because we're short-staffed at the moment, and in particular we don't have our own PF – Procurator Fiscal," he explained on seeing their puzzled looks, "there has been a delay in processing the findings from our initial investigation."

"Procurator Fiscal? Surely you only need one of those when there has been foul play?"

Max sounded surprised but Imogen interrupted, "I told you that someone suggested she may have been murdered," she reminded him.

"I'm really sorry but I can't go into any sort of detail here," Peterson continued, "and all I can tell you is that we will need to come to the house to look into one or two things. Will tomorrow afternoon be convenient?" He began to rise as if to leave.

"Erm…"

"Well…," they both began at once, "I think we need rather more information about what's going on," continued Max, "I'm really not very happy with the way things are being handled."

Peterson sighed deeply and sat down again, "I've told you all that I can. There are a few problems and we have several lines of enquiry to follow up on. There were no witnesses as far as we can tell, there's the significant injury to the victim's head, there's a lot of confusion about a missing key and finally the theft of your grandmother's car."

"Car?" cried the pair in unison, "Gran doesn't have a car!" exclaimed Imogen. Now it was Inspector Peterson's turn to look surprised, "But we caught the culprit red handed!"

"I can't help that," retorted Max, "the fact is my grandmother gave up driving over a year ago since her eyesight was beginning to fail. Did you think to check for a driving license?" he asked somewhat scathingly. "I don't know who you caught or whose car they were driving but it certainly wasn't Gran's."

Chapter 20

Manton

Inspector Peterson relaxed a little and appeared to be deep in thought before he looked up at the two expectant and surprised faces opposite him. He seemed to make a decision and then sat up straight, leant forward across the table and in a slightly conspiratorial manner began to explain,

"Our role here is mainly to gather information. This may seem insensitive but the more information we can get, the more we will understand the circumstances of a death. There may also be information that we cannot share with you; nothing personal but because it could harm any future prosecution."

Max and Imogen nodded in understanding and Peterson continued, "Sometimes we may need to keep some personal items belonging to the deceased person, for instance your Grandmother's wallet and car keys." He paused, "or whoever's key's they are! And we may need to ask you for personal details about her private life. We are not prying, it's just that the more we know about your loved one the more chance we have of identifying who committed the crime if indeed there was one. Of course, it may well have been an accidental death but we still need to go through the motions in order to rule out foul play."

Imogen's hand reached for Max's and he squeezed it comfortingly under the table.

"Unfortunately, we can't tell you how long any of this will take before we've completed our investigation and, as I indicated to you when I came in, we are currently rather short staffed and dealing with a larger than usual number of cases. Sometimes we are able to make an arrest very quickly but, in this case, although we have our suspicions, we are not yet ready to proceed. I can tell you that so far, we don't think there's sufficient evidence of murder as such but we are looking at a possible charge of culpable homicide. That's where loss of life is caused through wrongful conduct; where there was no intention to kill but a death happened as a result of recklessness. There's also the possibility that it's a case of diminished responsibility or mental illness. There are many aspects that we have to look into."

Peterson stopped. He looked up from his hands that he had stared at throughout, "I've told you much more than I should have," he said, "and much more than Arthur Lancer would have done, that's why we thought it best for him to act as go between, to sort of cushion the unpleasantness. However, since you've asked, I've told you. Now if you'll excuse me, I have an investigation to continue since I, as the senior officer here, have been appointed to look into these matters."

It being quite clear that the interview was now over, Imogen and Max thanked Peterson for his more than full explanation, agreed that he could come to the house the following afternoon and left the building with some relief and not a little bemusement. Gran murdered, accidentally or deliberately, either way it didn't bear thinking about!

In another room in the same police station, Otto Vasovich waited impatiently. It had been a very long few days. The overnight had become several nights and it appeared to be quite likely that it would become considerably longer than that. He was still completely bemused as to of what exactly he was suspected. He had already admitted to taking the car keys and driving the car without a license, insurance or any of the other prerequisites for so doing. Surely that didn't warrant keeping him here for so long? A fine, a ban, some other restrictions maybe but he hadn't intended to keep the car so it wasn't a theft – well certainly not in his opinion although he understood that it looked that way to others and of course, not speaking English made it very difficult to explain any of his side of things. The interpreter was helpful but she didn't really seem to understand everything he meant to say and the police didn't seem always to understand her. He certainly didn't understand them either.

The ladder? They kept going on about the ladder! He had tried to explain that when he first arrived at the churchyard, he saw a ladder lying across the path in a rather precarious position and posing a potential danger to anyone walking round the church. It was when he decided to move it to a safer place that he saw the handbag lying in the grass with its contents spilling out. There being no sign of any other person, although he could hear the mower on the far side of the church, and after repositioning the ladder against the wall, he gave in to temptation and took the car keys and the wallet that were in full view. He assumed that someone had inadvertently dropped the bag and would soon return to claim it and so he beat a hasty retreat, casting aside the now emptied wallet, and set off for a joy ride in the small car that he found parked a short distance from the church.

He knew he shouldn't have done it. He knew it would land him in trouble should he be caught, but he hadn't intended to harm anyone and the money he took was very little. It would have bought him a beer and a sandwich at the local pub; that's all. But he never made it to the pub. He was probably driving rather faster than was wise, in order to get as far from the church as possible before his misdeeds were discovered, and, some twenty minutes later, as he rounded a blind bend, he was obliged to swerve to avoid a woman on horseback. Unfortunately, that meant that he lost control of the little car for a moment or two and inadvertently caught a sharp rock with his front wheel. It was about ten minutes later when the punctured tyre brought him to an abrupt halt.

Apparently, the horsewoman had reported him for dangerous driving (damn cell phones – they made such tale-telling so much easier these days) and thus it was that the cops had found him and arrested him, resulting in his current unfortunate position. However, it didn't explain why they were holding him so long, why they were so interested in his repositioning of the dangerous, probably fallen, ladder or why they kept talking about serious charges, a dead lady and his potential deportation. Now that would be a complete disaster! How could he support his family with no job and no prospects? It had taken the last of his resources to come over here and work on Mr. Franklin's farm. Otto Vasovich put his head in his hands, and wept.

Chapter 21

The Manse

Reverend Bill was supposed to writing his sermon for next Sunday's service but his mind would not stay focused on the task in hand. The theme for his sermon was forgiveness; a topic that he regularly spoke about and which was often relevant in a small village where accusations and confrontations were rife. A close-knit community who knew each other well, made for gossip and back-biting within their ranks although, should an outsider attack any single one of them, the lines closed in and they would stand as one to defend their own. It was something of an anomaly which never ceased to puzzle Bill but which, over the years, he had come to accept as the norm for Hingemont folk.

Today, however, he was troubled. His involvement with Layla Lester was becoming a problem and he knew that he needed to take serious steps to end the affair. He felt guilty and disloyal to Mattie; the novelty and naughtiness was beginning to wear off and Layla herself was becoming too demanding and dangerously inappropriate. He couldn't bear for Mattie to find out and he had already been warned by Ada Springfield that tongues were wagging and that she knew what was going on. He had no doubt that she did – she was a busybody and a nosey parker but she could be trusted not to give him away because she had great respect for Matilda and for the Church. It would be a disgrace too far for him to be exposed as a cheat and a betrayer.

The little devil's voice in his head tempted him, telling him that Ada Springfield couldn't spill the beans on anyone now – she was dead after all… but no! If Ada had known, who else might be aware or suspect? They'd been careful, hadn't they? They had never been openly affectionate in public and their meetings had been discreet. Hadn't they? Bill continued to question himself. He thought he'd caught a glimpse of little Sammy in the old tree behind the school on more than one occasion and he remembered that one or two of the older school children had joked rudely about being able to see into Miss Lester's bedroom from that vantage point. What if…? It was a risk too far. He would tell Layla tonight that it had to stop. She wouldn't like it but that's how it must be… Ah! That gave him an idea and the sermon flowed from his fingers onto the screen in front of him; forgiveness of oneself would be the theme for this week.

Matilda sat on the kitchen stool in the room below where her husband was pondering his actions and his future. She stared at the dirty and crumpled piece of paper that she had found stuffed into the hedge next to her letter box. The misspelled and oddly formed words that were partially obscured due to the rain that had fallen overnight, made little sense to her and that which she could decipher didn't bear thinking about. "Yor mista woz wiv..." the next words were missing and then, "wich and eevl..." and finally, "exderminayt."

To read about her 'mista' and a 'wich', for some reason set alarm bells ringing in her head and her heart seemed to squeeze up very tightly in her chest. She wished she could simply dismiss the writing as some childish prank but she was suddenly uncomfortably aware of the doubts that had begun to creep into her daily life. There were the late homecomings, the odd direction of his approach on that one occasion, the excuses for needing to be out when she knew there were no meetings at the school or church and lastly, but not least, his recent coolness toward her and his lack of interest in the bedroom. She didn't want to think about it. She'd done her best to ignore her own doubts and misgivings. She wanted to trust Bill absolutely. But this...? What did it mean? There was no reference that she could decipher to any particular woman other than the word, 'wich' but, without prompting, Layla Lester popped into her mind and she was still sitting, immobile on the stool when that particular person knocked on her door.

Matilda nearly fell from the stool in her haste to hide the piece of paper and open the kitchen door. She was white-faced and trembling when she greeted the immaculately turned out school teacher who was smiling and friendly. Surely, she would not dare to come to the house like this if there were anything going on between her and Bill? Matilda

121

took a deep breath, dismissed her doubts and smiled back as she invited Layla into her kitchen.

Sometime later, arrangements for an old people's tea party confirmed and agreed, Layla left after hugging Matilda warmly and saying how grateful she was for her help. Matilda berated herself as she cleared away the debris from their tea and scones; how could she think such a thing of such a nice woman. Of course, the letter must have been referring to something else entirely and she, Mattie Banner, wife of the Reverend Bill Banner, was being silly and insecure to imagine he was anything other than totally faithful to her. He was just very busy and he worked so hard looking after the church, the school and all the villagers. She must try to do more to assist him.

As Layla Lester closed the gate to the Manse behind her, she looked up at the window above the kitchen. She could see Bill gazing out at her and she swung her hips provocatively as she sashayed down the road towards her cottage. What she didn't see was the look on Bill's face; a mixture of determination and devastation. He would not give in to temptation again but it could be extraordinarily difficult not to do so.

A short while later he made his way downstairs. He found Mattie up to her elbows in flour as she pounded furiously at the bread dough she was kneading. He made his way across the room and from behind her, wrapped his arms around her waist. She scolded him gently but leaned into his embrace and he kissed her neck. She turned and unheeding of the flour which was now liberally coating them both, she kissed him ardently. Surprised, he responded and quickly swept her off her feet and into the lounge where the old sofa awaited their passion. Whatever was he thinking betraying this loyal and loving wife for that 'chit of a girl' as his mother would have called her? No one could match Mattie as his partner, soul-mate and support. He had made the right decision. Layla wouldn't like it but Layla would have to lump it and accept that it was over. He was never again going to risk losing this woman who had stood by him for all these years. He loved her unconditionally.

Unseen by anybody, Sammy Jenkins crept along the hedgerow towards the Manse. He checked to see whether anyone was watching and having assured himself that no one was, he moved swiftly up to the pedestrian gate where the Manse letterbox hung lopsidedly. Pushing his hand into the hole in the hedge between the box and the gate-post, he nodded with satisfaction when he found the paper gone. It had been several days since he had pushed it in there and the recent rain had, until now, prevented him from checking whether it had been found. He hadn't wanted to put it in the letterbox because that might have meant that Rev Banner would find it. It wasn't meant for him and Mrs Banner was much more likely to remove a piece of paper from the hedge – she was a tidy person who was always picking litter out of the hedgerows. But gone it was, which meant it must have been found and if it had been found then surely it must have been read. Soon he would be rid of Miss Lester and her unfairness. Oh, how he hated her! With a smile he straightened up and skipped back down the road with lightness and hope in his step and in his heart.

Chapter 22

Hingemont House

Imogen was mildly disappointed, although not surprised, at Max's lack of interest in the love letters she had found. He was much more intrigued by the documented collection of knick-knacks and objets d'art that his grandfather had so painstakingly and carefully displayed – if indeed you could call the generally jumbled assortment a display. Despite the seemingly random placement of each item, there was an order to the mess. Each object had a small sticker attached upon which was printed a number and as he worked his way around the room, Max realised that the numbers ran consecutively from just inside the door and round to the left, that the numbered items on the shelves ran from top to bottom and by the time he had worked his way back to the right-hand side of the door he had reached number, three thousand, four hundred and nineteen. Checking in the ledger that was now on Grandpa's desk; open and accessible as a result of Matilda's tidying, he was able to identify some of the items by matching each number with the reference and description recorded in the book.

"Come and look at this!" he called to his sister, "who would have believed that the old man was this organised? I must admit that I always thought these things were just a lot of old junk but it seems that some of them at least have quite a significant value!"

Imogen left the letters she was reading, carefully replacing the ribbon around the pile, and made her way to where her brother pored over the ledger. "Hey!" he exclaimed, "there are some missing. Look, number forty-nine isn't there on the shelf and number sixty-four should be between that Cheshire dog and the porcelain doll. I wonder whether there are any more that have gone astray and, if so, where they could be."

"Well I've seen number forty-nine if it's that fake Fabergé egg thing," Imogen replied excitedly, "it's in Gran's room on her windowsill. Benjy very nearly knocked it off when I was in there looking for the will. I noticed a sticker on the bottom as I pushed it back into place but I didn't think anything of it. I wonder why Gran took that one."

"I expect she just liked it," Max replied, "and maybe it reminded her of Grandpa after he'd died. On the other hand, perhaps it isn't a fake after all and she took it up there for safe keeping." Imogen laughed saying, "We should be so lucky! Are there any more missing ones?"

"It will take me quite a long time to be certain but at the moment I can only identify one other and that should be a garden snail ornament. Number sixty-four, look here, it says, 'Large garden ornament in the shape of a snail, with removable shell revealing a chamber in which to place items for safety.'"

"Well I don't remember seeing anything like that around here," Imogen stood up to leave the room, "but it's time I fed Benjy and I should think you must be hungry too. It's been quite a day." Without further comment she left the room as Max continued to pore over the ledger, occasionally glancing up at the shelves in order to identify a specific item.

When Matilda Banner knocked on the kitchen door a little later that evening, Imogen noticed a lighter expression and a readier smile on her face and was pleased to accept an invitation to supper the following evening. She quickly explained that her brother was staying with her and Mattie immediately invited him as well. "Amy and her mother are coming too as well as Arthur Lancer and his mum. I hope you don't mind but we're having a little celebration and we thought it might cheer you up at this sad time. It will be our twenty-fifth wedding anniversary next week." she smiled broadly, "There will be a few other people from the village in attendance, such as Pamela Postlethwaite, Charlie – you remember him? And some old friends of ours who moved away a little while ago. I haven't asked Layla Lester yet but she's always so busy…" Matilda paused, a slight frown creased her brow, but then she rushed on gushingly, "I do hope you can come?"

Having assured her that she would be delighted to attend and that she was sure Max would be pleased to meet some of the villagers who may well remember him and his other siblings as young children, Imogen offered Mattie some refreshment but was inwardly rather relieved when the excitable lady refused saying she must hurry off to ensure that the other potential attendees were invited.

A little later, having taken Benjy for a quick walk round the nearby playing field, Imogen and Max relaxed into the comfy armchairs in Gran's lounge, and reminisced their childhood visits to Hingemont House; the adventures they had, the sleepless nights and scary stories, their fondness for Gran and Grandpa, the quirkiness of the old house and the seemingly never-ending supplies of love, hugs and strawberries.

"You know, it's strange to think that they're both gone," observed Max. "It seemed as though they would always be here... and that we would be young for ever... you don't think about growing up or growing old until it has happened and you can never go back to how it was..." Imogen broke into his reverie by throwing a cushion at him, "Speak for yourself old man!" she laughed, but then she stopped and found that her heart was in her mouth and tears were in her eyes, "Oh Gran," she sobbed, "I am going to miss you so much..."

"And murdered?" questioned Max, "I really find it impossible to believe that anyone would do such a thing..."

~

Matilda hesitated for a long while outside Layla's cottage. It would seem churlish not to invite her to the supper, and she really had no reason for not doing so. It was just a feeling, intuition perhaps, but she was uncomfortable around the head-teacher. She couldn't explain it and Bill obviously liked and approved of her, but she didn't fit in somehow. She was too flirtatious, too flippant and although she was a good teacher, she didn't quite fill the shoes of the previous incumbent and was nothing at all like sturdy Pamela Postlethwaite. Fighting with her own conscience, Mattie took a deep breath, pushed open the rickety gate and marched determinedly up to the door. Two sharp raps. Nothing. Another, slightly more tentative knock and then she almost jumped out of her skin when a small boy leapt out of the hedge and told her, "She ain't in. She's gawn to some witches' rally or somefink. I see'd her go about half an hour ago."

"Well thank you Sammy," breathed Mattie, as soon as she had regained her equilibrium, "I'll try again later perhaps."

"I woulden if'n I was you. She's evil that one!" opined Sammy.

"Now Sammy you shouldn't say such things about other people," Mattie began, but Sammy interrupted, "You would if you knew what I know and if'n you'd seen what I seed," he retorted, "Rev Bill knows about her too. I heard 'im trying to help 'er but no one ever listens ter me!" He folded his arms dramatically across his chest and stuck out his chin to demonstrate the importance of what he was saying and with that Matilda's resolve crumpled and she shooed Sammy home with a few more words of remonstration and a hand in the small of his back as she turned tail and scuttled home in the opposite direction as quickly as possible. The supper party would manage very well without Layla Lester in attendance.

Chapter 23

The Manse

One last look around the dining room confirmed to Matilda that all was in place; the cutlery, glassware, napkins and floral centrepiece, carefully positioned so as not to obscure anyone's view of the assembled guests, co-ordinated and sparkling, making for a very decorative table. One last tweak at the edge of the damask tablecloth and she hurried to check the oven before going upstairs to slip into a simple but elegant dress she'd laid out ready for the occasion.

Bill met her on the landing, coming down as she was going up and she tasked him with lighting the ready laid fire and the candles. He smiled at her excited eyes and swung her into his arms, giving her a fierce kiss as she chided him for ruffling her newly coiffed hair. But she leaned into him for a moment or two before pulling herself away and into the bedroom in order to change her clothes.

The first to arrive was Pamela who came bearing an enormous cake which was decorated with a silver 25 and emblazoned with 'Congratulations!' "It's from us all, but I made it myself!" she declared as she placed it carefully on the sideboard, "Everyone wanted to wish you well on your special day but of course there isn't room in here for the whole village!" Her glance swept round the room and took in the twelve place settings. "I expect we'll have a little celebration after the service on Sunday," she murmured and plonked herself down in the rocking chair set by the French window that led to the garden patio.

Next came Mary and Arthur Lancer, closely followed by Amy and Grace and by the time Grace's wheelchair had been carefully manoeuvred into the room, Imogen and Max were knocking at the door. Last to arrive were Queenie and Eric Dawn; who were great friends of the Banners. Queenie had been Matilda's bridesmaid and Eric was Bill's best man at the wedding twenty-five years ago. Although they had lived in Hingemont until quite recently, they had moved to another village a couple of years earlier. They confirmed that they knew everyone present and remembered Max and Imogen playing with their own children during their frequent visits to Gran and Grandpa at Hingemont House.

Before long everyone was chatting and reminiscing. The room buzzed with familiarity and cosy comfort. Tongues were loosened by fine sherry and the aroma that wafted from the kitchen bore the promise of good food to follow.

~

Making her way home from her late-night shopping trip, Layla slowed as she passed the brightly lit Manse. Good smells and convivial noises emanated from the opened windows and for a brief moment she wondered why she had not been invited to join the party. Then she remembered Bill's coolness toward her earlier that afternoon and a wry smile twisted her once pretty mouth. She knew that what they had shared was coming to its inevitable conclusion but she wasn't going to be the only victim to be hurt in the aftermath.

~

The excellent meal was eaten, the roast and garden grown vegetables, succulent and well-seasoned, were followed by a magnificent raspberry pavlova. There was no doubt that Mattie was an excellent cook. The assembled party had moved into the spacious lounge and were reclining on the comfortable sofas and armchairs, sipping their after-dinner coffee and waiting for their meal to have settled before cutting the much-admired cake when the gentle hum of conversation was rudely interrupted by a loud banging at the front door. All were silent as Bill made his way, perhaps a little unsteadily due to the fairly large quantity of wine he had supped with his meal, to see who had called at this rather inopportune moment.

His astonishment at the appearance of Inspector Peterson and MPC Carter on his doorstep must have shown in his face. He found himself automatically looking for Guinness, Carter's mount who was usually tethered to the gatepost when she came to call, before collecting himself, acknowledging that they would have arrived together in the black Mercedes that was parked outside The Manse, and enquired of them as to how he could be of assistance.

Having explained that they would like to ask him a few questions and having been told unequivocally that it could not wait, Bill invited them into his study and after closing the door a little more forcefully than was strictly necessary, sat down abruptly in his office chair. At first the officers were apologetic for having interrupted the evening but as they began to press Bill rather more strongly to explain his whereabouts on the day of Ada's death and in response to his somewhat vague replies, they became more insistent. Apparently, Layla Lester had claimed that she was with the Reverend, discussing some school and church matters and they needed him to verify the details. Having been put on the spot, and not thinking very clearly due to the combination of an unusually relaxed evening and a copious quantity of wine, Bill's uncharacteristic responses were vague and did little to relieve the concerns of the officers.

Inspector Peterson tapped his fingers impatiently on the edge of the bookcase against which he leant while Helen Carter asked once again, "So were you with Miss Lester or not?" Unfortunately, at precisely that moment, Mattie opened the door and overhearing the question; she turned pale, stumbled and dropped the tray of coffee mugs that she had brought for the extra guests. The ensuing chaos provided Bill with a short time to compose himself and to think more clearly about how to give an acceptable answer. Yes, he had been with Miss Lester, at a pre-arranged meeting in her home to discuss the future of the choir and the involvement of the school children in church services. His response seemed to satisfy the questioners who, much to Bill's consternation, then asked if they could interview some of the other guests, it being rather convenient to have many of the involved parties in the same place at the same time. Notwithstanding his annoyance at the hi-jacking of his celebratory party, Bill conceded to the common sense of the situation.

Matilda, struggling hard to control the tears that threatened to stream down her cheeks, quickly cleared up the spilt coffee and broken shards and ushered the unwelcome guests into the lounge where the assembled company greeted them with varying degrees of cordiality. Queenie and Eric were quickly dismissed as having no relevance to the enquiries and, realising that the evening was not going to pan out quite as expected, they made their apologies for an early departure, collected their coats, hugged Imogen, Max and Matilda and bade everyone farewell. They left carrying promises of another visit as soon as possible and slices of cake to be posted to them in due course. Mattie, having seen her dear friends out of the door and to their car, sniffed back her emotions and took in a deep breath of the cold evening air, before making her way back into the now subdued room.

There was no need for introductions since apart from Max and Imogen whom he had met earlier, all of the guests were familiar figures in Hingemont, Manton and Luttington but Inspector Peterson, demonstrating precisely why he had achieved his high rank, had noted an unused place setting at the dining table. His first question was an enquiry as to for whom the extra place had been prepared.

"For Charlie of course," replied Mattie, "I put an invitation through his letterbox yesterday and I was little surprised when he didn't reply or arrive tonight. Does anyone know where he is? I haven't seen him for a few days now." There followed a short silence until Helen cleared her throat and explained that Charlie was being held for questioning. Obviously reluctant to provide any more information, she was relieved that the need to explain further was drowned out by the clamour that followed her revelation. After a few moments, Peterson held up his hand and the room quietened as he assured all that Charlie was safe, that they didn't think he had done anything untoward but that he couldn't adequately explain the bloodied shovel he had been using or the blood on his hands and trousers. Charlie had been temporarily admitted to the safety of the psychiatric ward at Manton Hospital and was being treated for his stress and anxiety at having apparently been the first to discover Ada's body lying in the churchyard. Charlie's simplicity and ingenuous inability to lie meant that although there were some iniquities in his story, he wasn't any longer considered a suspect in the police enquiries.

In an inspired moment of clarity, Bill seized an opportunity to divert the attention from his dubious whereabouts. "I know Charlie very well," he began, "would it help if I came along to the hospital with you to see if he can tell me a bit more about that shovel and how he got blood all over the place?"

Chapter 24

Hingemont House

Imogen hugged her steaming mug of tea, knees drawn up under her chin and Benjy nestled under the arch that the raised legs provided. "What an incredible evening that was!" she remarked, "not at all what we were expecting."

"No indeed," replied Max, "you couldn't have written it in a book or film really. No one would have believed it. Especially when Mary and Grace got going…" Imogen chuckled at the memory of the two old ladies arguing over who was responsible for the mislaid key and their attempts to blame each other for poor Gran's demise. The mention of the snail had struck a chord though. Max and Imogen had looked at each other sharply as Mary explained that the key was hidden inside a snail but that the snail had gone missing. "Grandpa's snail," they had exclaimed together while the rest of the party looked at them in confusion. Imogen had quickly explained the catalogued collection and the missing number sixty-four, a large garden ornament, in the shape of a snail. Had the snail been where it was supposed to have been, none of the events of that fateful afternoon would have occurred. Charlie would not be in hospital, Otto would not be in jail, Max would be at home with his wife and children and she,

Imogen, would be... where would she be? She suddenly realised that she was actually rather pleased to be here. Obviously, it would all be much better if Gran were here too, but on the whole, she was happier here than she'd been anywhere else for a very long time.

There had been another enlightening revelation during the enquiries that evening. Mary explained that it was her car that had been taken. She had driven to the church but had left her keys with Gran whilst she walked to the village store to ask whether they had a spare church key. In the melee that followed on her return, she had completely forgotten about her car and it was only much later that she wondered its whereabouts. By that time, it had been found, Otto Vasovich had been arrested for speeding and theft and the car impounded for forensic investigation. There was also much speculation that Otto had been responsible for Ada's death; no specific details of what had happened were revealed and enquiries were significantly hindered by Otto's lack of English. The interpreter did her best, but some words just did not translate adequately and so progress was slow. In the meantime, Inspector Peterson had explained, Otto would be held on suspicion of murder, car theft and other associated crimes, until such time as they could ascertain exactly how Gran had met her unfortunate demise.

On the whole it was all very unsatisfactory. However, the coroner having already confirmed that the cause of death was a blow to the head and having also completed further necessary forensic examination, had decreed that the body could be released for disposal. Disposal? Such an unfortunate and undignified end to a very full and vibrant life. Poor Gran. Imogen was determined that she would organise as good a celebration of Gran's life as possible under the circumstances and that was her starting point for today.

Uncurling her legs and returning the now empty mug to the kitchen sink, she hurried to dress and prepare for a day of visits to the funeral parlour, a florist, Bill Banner, to organise a memorial service, and the crematorium to arrange a time and date for that necessary committal. Max was tasked with collecting memories from various members of the family and the community and was to begin collating them into some semblance of a suitable obituary. It was going to be a long day...

~

Matilda found it extremely hard to bring herself to even get out of bed the morning after her anniversary. She would like to have explained her lethargy by suggesting that it followed a night of celebratory passion but the truth was the absolute opposite. Although she and Bill had retired to their bedroom soon after the final guest had left – she had begun to think that Pamela Postlethwaite would never leave – neither of them had been able to sleep. After lying in silence, next to each other, not touching, for almost an hour, Bill had sighed

140

deeply, muttered something about needing water, and had got out of bed and disappeared. Mattie lay there a little longer, willing herself to fall asleep, but eventually she too got up, drew her fleecy gown around her shoulders and made her way down into the darkened lounge. A little glimmer of light emanated from the embers in the fireplace and she pulled an armchair closer to the fireplace.

She wasn't sure how long she sat there mulling over the events of the evening; going over and over the conversations that had taken place. She dwelt on the overheard remarks about Layla Lester and her husband's whereabouts, she pondered on the discussion of Charlie's possible involvement, on Otto Vasovich's wrongdoings and on the disappearance of the snail and the key. None of it made any sense and she was angry at the ruination of her carefully planned party. This was supposed to have been a celebration of twenty-five happy years but now she found herself doubting the happiness, questioning her husband's fidelity, suspicious of motives and movements that she had never considered before. Tears rolled down her cheeks and she angrily brushed them away, her anger aimed at herself for her foolish naivety and her blind faith in her husband, her neighbours and even God. Eventually weariness overcame her anger and she crawled up the stairs and into her bed. She didn't remove her dressing gown but held it tightly around her still shaking form until she slept.

Bill sat in his office chair and for the umpteenth time asked himself how he could have been so stupid as to jeopardise his marriage and the happiness of his wife, his position in the community and the trust that his congregation demonstrated in their constancy to him and the church. He was a fool and he knew it. He had already decided to end things with Layla and had made it clear to her earlier that same day, but he didn't trust her not to cause trouble. If she felt slighted by his change of heart, she had more than enough evidence to ruin him. He remembered how old Ada Springfield had tried to warn him. She had never explicitly accused him of any wrongdoing but what she had said had been enough to make him realise that she knew more than she was letting on.

He sat up suddenly and clapped his hands to his head, "My God!" he exclaimed, "that could be interpreted as motive for murder. I could have done it to shut her up! Did I? Am I so crazy that I could have done something like that and not know it? Does anyone else know what Layla and I were up to? Did Ada know about someone else's peccadilloes? Was Otto Vasovich up to no good? What about Charlie? Surely not... He's far too innocent despite his age..." Bill's thoughts whirled around in increasingly wild circles until sleep also overcame him and his head fell forward onto his outstretched arms, his eyes closed and his snores reverberated through the small room. However, there was no one to hear him, and only his nonsensical dreaming to disturb his slumber.

It was there, still sleeping, that Matilda found her husband when she eventually dragged herself out of bed and down the stairs the following morning.

Chapter 25

The Manse

The telephone rang shrilly, breaking the uncanny silence that filled the old house. No radio, no humming from Matilda as she set about preparing a cooked breakfast. Best cure for a hangover, she'd heard somewhere. Inexperienced in these matters, she tried to do her best for her husband. No whistling from upstairs as Bill prepared for another day of visiting the sick and elderly, attending functions and generally going about doing God's good works.

Matilda dropped the wooden spatula and grabbed the phone from its cradle on the wall, "Hello, Hingemont Manse," she said in automatic response.

"Hi Mattie, it's me," came Queenie's voice from the receiver, "I was a bit worried about you yesterday evening. You didn't seem quite yourself – especially after those officers gate-crashed your lovely party. I wondered if you would like to meet up so we can have a chat?"

Mattie found tears running down her cheeks and for a moment she couldn't speak at all. "Mattie? Are you there?" Queenie spoke softly, "Shall I come now? I could be there in about forty-five minutes."

"No, it's okay," sniffed Matilda, "I'm fine. Your kindness just took me by surprise. I don't know why I'm crying really; everything's fine..." But everything wasn't fine and the thought of being able to speak aloud her fears and concerns to her best friend in the whole world, had opened the floodgates of her too long suppressed emotions. Before much longer it was arranged that later in the afternoon, Matilda would meet Queenie at a Garden Centre on the edge of the nearby town of Wendle, where there was a newly opened café and where they could talk to their hearts content without fear of being overheard. That was a problem with living in such a small community; everyone knew everyone else's business, sometimes even before you knew it yourself!

Disturbed by the ring of the telephone and his wife's voice, Bill awoke. Stiff with his uncomfortable sleeping position and crumpled attire, head aching and thirsty, he stumbled into the kitchen and greeted his wife with a perfunctory peck on her cheek. He tasted the salt of her tears but his still befuddled brain didn't interpret the sign of her distress and he muttered something about washing and changing before gratefully accepting her thoughtful breakfast.

It was only after he had eaten, drunk his second cup of coffee and scanned the newspaper headlines, that he remembered his promise to visit Charlie. He would have to fit it in to his busy schedule but the meeting with Layla could wait and he wasn't at all sure that he wanted to see her right now anyway. Damn the woman!

Once again, the telephone rang. "Hingemont Manse," said Bill, and on hearing a female voice he turned a little pale. However, on recognising Imogen's tone, he quickly regained his equilibrium and agreed to meet up with her after he had seen Charlie. Oh, it was easy to fill his days and avoid seeing those parishioners he would prefer not to come into contact with. Even when this particular parishioner was desperate to see him. Of course, he would have to see her at some point. It was not possible for the vicar of the village church to completely avoid the head teacher of the village school. It was inevitable and imperative that they work together. Damn it!

Matilda and Bill went their separate ways. There would be time enough for discussion and explanation in the evening once the busy day was completed. Bill knew that he had a lot of explaining to do and not a little apologising and Matilda was anxious for reassurance and affirmation of their continued togetherness. First, however, they each had much to do on this fine autumnal morning.

~

Bill found Charlie slumped in an armchair in the day lounge of the rather impersonal psychiatric ward. At first Bill thought he was asleep but when he placed his hand on Charlie's shoulder, his eyes flew open and he sat up with a start.

"Bill! What are you doing here?" he mumbled, "can you take me 'ome?" and he began to scramble to his feet.

"No, sorry old boy," said Bill, "Not this time. I've come to see if you're okay. Make sure they're treating you well and to see if there's anything you need?"

"On'y ter get out of 'ere!" grumbled Charlie, "What about my work, the grass'll be up to me knees and weeds everywhere…" he opined.

"You mustn't worry about that sort of stuff," Bill replied, "the important thing is that you are well and stop being upset about what happened." He tried to keep it simple, not to expand on the horror that poor Charlie had found; he didn't want to stir up Charlie's reactions again. But Charlie was agitated and began to get loud, "They keep goin' on about me bloody shovel!" he said, "an' I tell 'em it were a brocken brock. It weren't nothin' ter do with the ole lady. They tell me I'm simple – well I tell you it's them that are. They just don' get it do them."

Bill, a bit shocked by Charlie's apparent understanding of his generally accepted simplicity - I suppose in polite society he would be described as autistic or mentally disabled. Although I think even that term is frowned upon nowadays. But to hear him call himself simple was entirely unexpected and implied a much greater understanding than Bill would have given him credit for. Resisting the instinctive rebuttal of Charlie's self-analysis, Bill

147

focussed on the bloody shovel and asked Charlie to expand on what he meant by a brocken brock. No wonder the police officers were confused! It sounded like a foreign language even to Bill.

"A brocken brock." Charlie said again, even more emphatically, "it were under the 'edge right behind Gertrude Foster's headstone. It were fresh and I had ter move it before it got smelly and attracted the flies. It were brocken alright. Prob'ly a car or summat." Suddenly realisation dawned and Bill exclaimed, "Oh! You mean a dead badger?"

"Tha's what I said, a brocken brock. I bin tellin' 'em that for days now!" Charlie was almost distraught with frustration but was at least a little relieved that Bill had understood him at last. A few minutes later, the mystery of the blood on the shovel, Charlie's hands and his clothes was solved; the badger was freshly dead and still soft with no rigor mortis. Consequently, it had slipped from the shovel and Charlie had been obliged to carry it in his arms to the hole that he had dug in readiness for its disposal. He had been on his way to return the shovel to the shed when he'd discovered poor Ada. He hadn't touched her; he hadn't done anything other than sound the alarm by shouting hysterically and wielding the bloodied shovel over his head before dropping into the grass where Helen Carter had found it.

A passer-by, somewhat alarmed by this apparent mad-man, waving wildly, covered in blood and incoherent in his attempts to draw attention to whatever was troubling him, had quickly whisked out her mobile phone and made the call that had summonsed Helen Carter on that fateful afternoon. The stranger hadn't waited to see how the events unfolded. She was much too affrighted by the gesticulating, inarticulate mad-man. The rest of the events of that day are already known to you.

It just so happened that shortly before Bill contacted Inspector Peterson to tell him the outcome of his visit to Charlie, a brown envelope containing a forensic report on the bloodied shovel and clothes, landed on Peterson's desk. Upon opening it, he discovered the welcome news that the blood was not human and was definitely not Ada Springfield's.

Chapter 26

Wendle

Queenie was already seated at an outside bench in the newly opened garden centre cafe when Matilda arrived. A little flustered and a little later than she had intended, she hurried through the building and out to greet her friend. Why was there always so much to do and so many delays when something important was looming? And yet when there is nothing in particular to get to grips with, time drags. Sod's law she supposed...

There was no hiding her distress from Queenie who had been her closest friend since their early days at the village school, their days of teenage angst and their rather wilder days attending college before their paths parted in early adulthood. Queenie had set off to Africa as a volunteer teacher, where she had met and later married Eric. On their return to the UK they had settled near Cambridge and had raised their three children; two sons and a daughter, all of whom were currently studying further afield, leaving Queenie free to pursue her former intention to become a counsellor and social support worker. She had always been the one to whom colleagues and peers turned for advice and comfort. She had an innate ability to know when help was needed and a common-sense approach to providing reassurance and sympathy without patronising or overbearing control.

Before long, Mattie and Queenie were laughing and reminiscing; all thoughts of the reason for their coming together appeared to have been forgotten. In actuality, neither of them had dismissed the real reason for their meeting but it was important to create a comfortable and safe environment for hearts to be opened and fears discussed. After a few, "Do you remembers..." and one or two, "How could we forget about..." followed by hysterical laughing about the time Queenie had lost her shoe when stepping down from a bus, suddenly Mattie's tears of laughter turned to tears of misery and without hesitation Queenie left her seat on the opposite side of the bench and came to fling her arms around her best friend's shoulders. She waited in silence until the initial onslaught had abated before gently prompting, "Tell me..."

It all came spilling out; how ever since old Ada Springfield's body had been found in the churchyard everything seemed to have become uncertain, upsetting and the natural equilibrium of Hingemont village had been thoroughly disturbed. Everyone seemed to be suspicious of somebody else; no one seemed to be acting in their habitual way and even the weather had turned cold and autumnal much sooner than expected. Finally, Matilda found the words to express her fears about Bill and Layla. At first Queenie was dismissive,

"Bill? Unfaithful to you? Never! He adores you..." but gradually, as Mattie explained her reasoning and, reluctantly, her 'evidence', Queenie became quieter and more thoughtful, "Well, I suppose it could be true... Layla Lester is certainly an attractive woman... and they have had plenty of opportunity... Oh Mattie! What are you going to do?"

"I suppose I have to confront him with it," she whispered, "but I don't think I want to know the answer..." she sniffed mightily and dabbed ineffectually at her tear streaked cheeks.

"Then don't ask him!" Queenie declared, "If you don't want to know and you love him, as I know you do, what good would it do to know the truth? Sometimes it's better to go on believing what we want to believe and in time, it will become reality. I don't think Bill wants to lose you and from what you say, anything that may have happened may already be over. You don't have to interact with Ms Lester any more than absolutely necessary and only on a business level. Make it clear to her somehow that you suspect something untoward has been going on and that you won't tolerate her interference in your marriage. There are ways of saying things without actually saying it – if you know what I mean?"

"Yes." Mattie responded a little more optimistically, "That's what I was afraid of – that if I faced him with my fears, I would drive him away from me but I didn't think of approaching it the other way round! It would be much easier to show Layla that I won't stand for any nonsense! Thank you my dear friend – you're always so sensible!"

"Oh I don't know about that!" replied Queenie with a sheepish grin, "There was a time when I was rather suspicious of Eric and his attractive secretary. Once when I went to his office I saw their heads unnecessarily close together and I jumped to a conclusion. The next time I saw her, a few days later, I took her a cup of coffee which 'accidently' spilled into her lap necessitating a trip to the bathroom to mop her up. I told her in no uncertain terms that Eric and I had a wonderful relationship and that no one in the world could ever come between us. She turned an unattractive shade of beetroot and muttered something unintelligible before giving me a rather stiff hug and mumbling an apology – at least I think that's what it was but I don't really want to know. She left the firm the following week!"

A little while later, after another cup of tea and a currant bun apiece, Queenie and Mattie parted company with promises to keep in touch better than they had recently and an agreement to meet once a month for a good chat, tea and sympathy if necessary.

~

Sammy had been missing all day. Performing one last check at the end of school, Pamela Postlethwaite found him huddled in a corner of the boy's cloakroom. Before she could ask him what he

153

was doing hiding in there after school, he flung himself into her arms, sobbing, "Don' make me go back in 'er class Ma'am. She's evil and I 'ate 'er!"

"There, there," Pamela soothed as she swept him up in her ample bosom, "Let's mop you up and find you somewhere more comfortable to sit and tell me what's troubling you."

When Sammy had finished explaining what he had seen and heard, Pamela was in no doubt as to exactly what he had witnessed although she was careful not to tell him what it was all about. She soothed and reassured him that Ms Lester was not a witch and that he had misunderstood what he had observed. She emphasised that it was important not to jump to conclusions when you aren't in possession of all the facts and details. She gave him squash and biscuits, rumpled his hair and mopped his tears in her inimitable motherly style before bundling him into her car and driving him the short distance to his home. She left him with his Grandmother and suggested he should be kept at home for a day or two while she sorted things out at school. Before leaving, she hugged Sammy tight and promised things would be better when he returned on Monday next week. He smiled wetly and thanked her but his parting shot was, "If'n I 'ave ter be in 'er class, I'm not comin'!"

Pamela Postlethwaite was on the war path – and she was not going to pull her punches!

Chapter 27

Otto Vasovich

A few miles away, in an uncomfortable holding cell, which to most people would have been unbearably stark and bare, Otto Vasovich, despite his misgivings about his future, continued to almost enjoy the quiet of the confined space. He had been fed, had a pillow and a blanket and was warm which for him was somewhat unusual. The barn dormitory at Layton had not been exactly comfortable and was decidedly draughty as well as noisy at times. Nevertheless, despite his situational content, Otto really wanted to know how long he was to be kept in this place. He fully understood that he had done wrong in taking the car, the money from the fallen wallet and had driven much too fast and without a license but he really didn't understand what he was being accused of with regard to the old lady.

The interpreter had explained to him that they were trying to ascertain what had happened to her and that somehow he was involved. For the life of him (and it seemed it could be a lifetime) he didn't understand what they wanted him to tell them. They kept asking about a ladder and he repeatedly told them he had left it leaning against the church wall. "Kopėčios buvo atsirėmusios į sieną." However, it seemed his answer didn't satisfy them and they

155

asked him again and again, "Where was the ladder?"

"Prieš siena."

"Where was the lady's body?"

"Nežinau." (I don't know)

"What did you hit her with?"

"Aš niekam nepataikiau." (I didn't hit anyone)

"Why did you take the car?"

"Aš tiesiog norėjau važiuoti," (I just wanted to go for a drive) and round they would go in circles, the same questions and the same replies over and over. Otto was quite sure they wanted him to confess to something he hadn't done but he was completely unable to make them understand that he simply wanted to feel a sense of freedom and normality for the brief period of his unexpected afternoon off.

His quiet reverie was rudely interrupted as Inspector Peterson unlocked the cell door and indicated that Otto should follow him into the nearest interview room.

Much to his surprise, Otto recognised one of the fellow workers from Layton Farm and he greeted him warmly. Igor did not return the same warmth of greeting and avoided making eye contact as he grunted a perfunctory, "Sveiki."

Clearly, he was not happy to be there and was possibly even less happy to be involved in whatever mess it was that Otto was tangled in. Nevertheless, his grasp of English was rather better than the interpreter's understanding of Lithuanian and the promise of a beer or two had persuaded Igor to come to the aid of his co-worker.

It was surprising to Otto just how quickly the misunderstanding was cleared up. Through Igor's translation skills, the business of the ladder and Otto's witnessing of the scene he came across on that unfortunate afternoon was soon explained...

Otto had entered the churchyard from the road side of the building, through the lych-gate where we previously found Helen Carter and Guinness. Making his way round the church, he first came across a ladder which was lying on the ground. Since it was inhibiting his progress, and that of anyone else who may have wished to follow the path, he replaced it against the church wall from whence he assumed it had fallen. His next find was the apparently discarded handbag and its spilled contents which included the wallet from which he took some money, and the car keys that led to his ultimate downfall and current situation. As to the body, which he now understood had been lying nearby; he knew nothing since he hadn't seen it. He had hurried away with the money and the keys for fear of being caught taking something that was not his. How ironic was that now?

Much to his relief, Otto soon found himself being taken back to Layton Farm. Igor was no more friendly on the journey back than he had been on his arrival but later that evening, after several bottles of beer in the farm canteen, he flung his arm across

Otto's shoulder and muttered thickly, "Kitą kartą, kai jūs pateksite į šūdą, neateikite pas mane jūsų išvežti!" (next time you get into some shit, don't come to me to haul you out!) He slapped Otto hard on the back and then roared with laughter whilst bragging to the assembled company that he was going to change his job from hard labour to court translator!

As soon as he could reasonably slip away, Otto retired to his bunk in the draughty dormitary and pondered on how he was going to raise the money to pay his speeding fine. There were no points to be added to his non-existent license in this country and a ban from driving was no hardship to one who didn't have access to a vehicle. All in all, and under the potentially disastrous circumstances, he thought he had probably got off rather lightly.

~

Arthur Lancer leant back in his office chair and pondered on the strange conversation he had just had with Amy. He had to admit to himself that he was becoming increasingly enamoured with the girl and was very anxious not to say or do anything to upset the applecart. He realised there was a rather large age gap and perhaps he was kidding himself by thinking they could be anything more than colleages or good friends. Certainly she had seemed uncomfortable in her haste to leave the office after their chat. What was that all about? She had turned rather pale and looked anxious before abruptly telling him she had to go home immediately. What

158

could have prompted her sudden change of attitude? After all, they had only been discussing Inspector Peterson's most recent revelation about the nature of the blood on Charlie's shovel. Was she squeamish perhaps? Women! Arthur began to think that maybe they are more trouble than they are worth and he would be better off forgetting all about the possibility of another relationship. After all, he and his mother rubbed along quite comfortably and it was all very uncomplicated that way.

~

Amy wasn't sure whether to laugh or to cry! Why hadn't her mother said anything about the little incident she'd had on that fateful day? Could she really have forgotten all about it? Amy supposed that was possible given the extraordinary circumstances but the blood on her scooter was irrefutable evidence wasn't it? Although it had puzzled her at the time she washed the scooter, Amy hadn't given it much more thought until Arthur informed her of the badger blood on Charlie's shovel.

Poor Charlie had suffered greatly and most unfairly from the lack of information and there was an air of doubt and mistrust hanging over the whole of Hingemont because of the intrigue and half truths that were being revealed. If only Grace had mentioned that she had hit a badger on her way to the church there would have been no need for Charlie's incarceration in the phsyciatric ward and another small piece of the complicated puzzle would have slotted into place.

Amy hurried home to confront her mother and settle any residual doubt about how the poor badger came to be dead and buried in the churchyard. Perhaps Grace knew more than she was letting on about the missing snail too? Amy wouldn't put it past her mother to have tried to confuse her elderly friends by playing such a prank on them. There was nothing she enjoyed more than other peoples' discomfiture.

Chapter 28

Hingemont House

The date was set, the arrangements made, the guests invited. All that remained was for Imogen to tidy the rest of the house, prepare the guest rooms for those who needed to stay; especially her mother, and to ask Matilda to help her with providing food for her house guests.

Caterers had been hired for the wake which was to be held in the ballroom of Partington Hall. Imogen had been astonished to discover that the ballroom still existed, largely unaltered for a great many years. Amy explained that it hadn't been used for as long as she could remember but that her mother insisted on keeping it in good order. The floor was regularly polished, the chandeliers cleaned and the hangings aired once a year every summer. It was a little piece of history encapsulated in Partington Hall and only needed the hiring of some chairs and banqueting tables to make it an eminently suitable venue for the celebration of Ada's life. No doubt she had danced there in her youth, perhaps she had even met Grandpa on one of those occasions? Imogen and Max were delighted to accept Grace's generous offer and the old lady was only too pleased to be able to make small recompense for the delay she had inadvertently caused by omitting to mention the incident with the badger!

There was just one week to go before the day of Gran's memorial service - a celebration of her life – no tears – just happy memories. But Imogen couldn't help feeling that it would be so much easier to celebrate her life if they actually knew how she had met her death. Accordingly she had arranged to meet with Inspector Peterson at Arthur Lancer's office later that afternoon in the hopes that he may be able to provide some answers.

~

Mattie welcomed Imogen into her homely kitchen and was delighted to be of assistance with providing for Ada's family. Imogen explained that her brothers and their families, her mother and one of her cousins would be staying for the weekend and could Mattie help with a menu and some of the cooking? Mattie wouldn't just help, she would provide everything from the menu to the cooking, the serving and the clearing away but could she ask her friend Queenie to come and help her?

"Oh my goodness!" exclaimed Imogen, "surely that's just too much?" but Mattie was insistent and it was soon agreed that Queenie would come to help and Imogen could leave all the arrangements to the two of them. All she needed to do was to let Mattie know who was arriving and when, and how long they would be staying. Imogen was astonished at the generosity of her new found friends and was beginning to think that she never wanted to leave this little village. Time would tell...

~

Arthur welcomed Max and Imogen into his office and invited them to sit and take coffee whilst they awaited the arrival of Insptector Peterson. Imogen refused politely but Max accepted the offer. Forgetting that Amy had left for the afternoon, Arthur pressed the buzzer and tutted to himself when she didn't respond. He would have to make the coffee himself. However, on reaching the small kitchen area, he was pleasantly surprised to discover that Amy had had the foresight to leave a flask of coffee ready made for his appointees. There was also a packet of his favourite biscuits; custard creams, thoughtfully left out where he could see them with a clean plate ready on which to serve them. "She really is a keeper; this Amy!" he thought to himself for the umpteenth time!

Inspector Peterson arrived, a little late as usual, and entered in his usual brisk manner. After refusing coffee he began, "I've agreed to meet you and update you on our progress so far but I have to warn you that I don't have any concrete answers for you just yet. We have, however, been able to rule out a few possibilities and it's becoming increasingly clear that we don't have much evidence for foul play. Most of our lines of enquiry have come to a dead end – if you'll excuse the pun – and so for the time being we're going to work on the premise that there's been some sort of accident, or perhaps a series of unfortunate events." He held up his hand to stem the interruption from Max, "I'll take questions when I've finished, he said curtly before continuing, "You'll be pleased to know, no doubt, that Charlie Evans, the groundsman, has been cleared and will be going home from the hospital tomorrow. Bill Banner has arranged to collect him and settle him back in his own home and that foreign chap, Otto somethingorother, although he's been charged with theft and dangerous driving, is now back at the farm where he's employed. We had other suspicions, as you know, and surprisingly there were one or two people who may have had a motive for murder." Here he looked hard at Arthur who turned a little pale but didn't lower his gaze in return, "and for a time we thought the two other older ladies might have had some sort of grudge to bear. But it seems their differences were all pretty superficial and certainly not enough to make either of them want to see Mrs Springfield dead

Once again an interruption was attempted, this time from Imogen, but she got no further than, "But..." when Peterson's hand was again raised in objection and he glared at her, "All in good time," he repeated and went on, "There was animal blood on a shovel, as I'm sure you know, but there was also blood on a rock not far from where the bo..., sorry, your Gran, was lying when we found her. We've sent a sample from the rock to forensics to determine whether it was the same' blood or from someone or something else. We haven't yet received a conclusive result but we're anticipating a match." Max was astonished that this point hadn't been investigated much earlier in the proceedings, however, he realised that out here in the countryside things progressed rather more slowly than they did in the big cities. Manton was very small fry compared with his home town. He must remember to be patient.

Peterson took a deep breath in preparation for continuing but at this point the phone rang and, excusing himself, Arthur answered it. He looked both surprised and pleased before saying gruffly, "I think it might be best if you could come to the office immediately. How long will it take you to get here?" He nodded to the assembled company before ending the call, replacing the receiver and saying, "That was Amy; she has something important to tell you Inspector. She'll be here in about twenty minutes. I hope you can wait that long?" Peterson glanced at his wristwatch and tutted before agreeing that he could spare another half an hour but no more.

Chapter 29

Hingemont

Grace was absolutely furious. How dare they confiscate her scooter! How was she supposed to get around without it and how long did they think they were going to inconvenience her for?

Amy did her best to console her irate mother and explained that it would only be for a day or two until they could verify the source of the stains on the front bumper.

"If only you'd told me you'd hit something I wouldn't have worried about washing the mark off but after the accident had happened and there was blood being talked about, I realised that was what it was and I was concerned that I had inadvertently concealed or destroyed some vital piece of evidence. I had to tell someone and Arthur said I should tell Inspector Peterson. So I did. It's a good job modern forensics are so advanced and they think they can find out what the stain was despite my best attempt to scrub it clean!"

Grace harrumphed and glared at her daughter who bade her goodnight and quietly left her mother's bedroom. Grace was beginning to wish she hadn't offered her ballroom for Ada's reception; that would show Amy who was in charge around here – perhaps she could rescind the offer? She was on the point of ringing the little bell on her bedside

166

table to summons Amy back and tell her so, when she stopped and looking at the photograph of herself, Ada and Mary, she sighed deeply and realised just how unreasonable she was being. A tear trickled down her wrinkled cheek and she made no attempt to brush it away as she breathed deeply and pondered how greatly everything had changed since that fateful afternoon.

The last thought that flitted through her mind as she gave in to the inevitable effect of her sleeping tablet was, 'I wonder where that blasted key is? I don't remember anyone saying it has been found yet!"

~

Layla Lester was puzzled. There had been a complete turnaround in Bill Banner's behaviour towards her. He ignored her at every opportunity and barely spoke to her when there was no avoiding her. What could she have done to have caused such a dramatic change? She hadn't meant to fall in love with him. It had only ever been a bit of a fling; a release of pent up tension, although she had to admit that he was a very attractive man. But she knew she had been playing with fire. He was married and a clergyman; how much more dangerous (and exciting) could it be to seduce such a man? Oh he'd been ready enough to accommodate her desires. No wonder with a frump of a wife such as Matilda although she had to admit that Mattie had a heart of gold even though she had also been avoiding Layla recently.

Layla sighed and pushed aside the pile of books she had been marking. She downed the last of the large glass of wine she had been sipping and determined that she would confront Bill tomorrow. He would have to come to the school for the usual Monday morning assembly and she had a spare half an hour straight afterwards; half an hour in which it had been their custom to make a quick visit to the school house. No doubt that wouldn't happen tomorrow, judging by the current state of affairs. She wondered again about the dinner party to which she hadn't been invited but dismissed her feelings of rejection and put it down to her still being an outsider as far as the villagers were concerned. How strange it is that one has to have been resident in a village for at least a dozen years before one was accepted as 'belonging'.

~

The following morning, Layla was extremely surprised when Bill arrived at school, just in time for the assembly, accompanied by his wife. Layla settled the pupils in the small hall and provided a seat for Matilda beside Pamela Postlethwaite before unnecessarily introducing Bill to the children. "Good morning Reverend Banner," they all chanted in sing-song unison.

"Good morning children," he replied. "Now I'm going to talk to you this morning about telling the truth," he began and the children all nodded wisely and looked from one to another while some shuffled nervously on their bottoms. "You all know how very important it is to always tell the truth no matter what. Can anyone tell me why that is?"

Sammy Jenkins' hand shot up and without waiting to be asked he yelled, "Cos if'n you tell a lie ain't no one goin' ter believe yer next time." Layla was about to remonstrate with Sammy for calling out when Pamela calmly interjected, "Well done Sammy, quite right, but perhaps you shouldn't speak until you're asked?"

"Sorry," said Sammy gruffly and added under his breath, "Don't make much difference if'n you do tell the truth, ain't no one going ter believe you anyways." It seemed that he hadn't entirely got over his upset from the previous week but Mrs Postlethwaite had promised to help and he was prepared to give her a chance.

After a brief but pointed lecture about the importance of trust and how easily it could be destroyed, some of which the children understood but much of which was entirely lost to their young minds, Layla wondered for whom exactly the message was intended. It seemed too much of a coincidence that Bill happened to choose that particular topic following the confusion of the previous week.

Making her way to her office she was further surprised to see not only Bill and Mattie but Pamela also waiting outside her door. She invited them in and offered them coffee before realising that she must make it herself since her secretary who doubled as a teaching assistant, would be minding the children while Pamela was not in the classroom. She quickly produced four mugs, a steaming kettle and a plate of biscuits and soon they were all amicably, or so it seemed, sipping and munching.

"Thank you for your talk this morning," Layla began but Pamela interrupted, "I'm only here for a few minutes," she said, "but I need to tell you that I have arranged for Sammy Jenkins to be with me until the end of this term. He's been very upset and unhappy for some time and I think it's best if I keep an eye on him until he's sorted himself out."

"Oh!" exclaimed Layla, taken aback at the unprecedented display of authority from her colleague, "Do you know why he's been so unhappy?" she asked.

"Yes I do," replied Pamela, "but I'm not going to discuss it with you right now. Maybe not ever; I think you've got enough problems to sort out at the moment so if you'll excuse me I have a lesson to deliver." She rose to leave, smiled briefly at Matilda and scowled at Bill before closing the door behind her with a very definite bang.

There was an uncomfortable silence in the room for a few minutes until Matilda rose abruptly from her chair, mug in hand and advanced deliberately toward Layla. "Thank you for the coffee and thank you for all you have done for Bill over the past few months but I want you to be among the first to know that he won't be able to spend so much time at the school from now on. We've accepted a special commission from the archbishop and we'll be working together on a series of sermons for the various lay preachers to deliver at services in the village churches. We are going to be very busy." At this point, she had reached Layla's side and as she reached out to place her mug on the work surface behind Layla's chair, she jogged Layla's elbow. Layla's mug flew out of her hand and into Bill's lap, the dregs soaking his trousers in a most inappropriate place. Layla leapt to her feet but before she could grab a handful of paper towels, Mattie spun her around to face her and hissed at her, "I think you'll find that's my prerogative. My husband, my mistake..." and then, much more quietly, so that only Layla could hear, "and I'll thank you to leave him to me from now on."

There was absolutely no doubt about the message behind Mattie's words and Layla blushed and stammered incoherently but neither Bill nor Matilda heard what she was trying to say since, hand in hand, they left the building without a backward glance.

Chapter 30

Hingemont

Queenie and Mattie chuckled to themselves as they were busy in Mattie's kitchen, preparing dishes for Imogen's guests.

"You should have seen her face!" laughed Mattie. "Talk about embarrassed!"

"But it worked didn't it?" asked Queenie.

"Oh yes it certainly did!" replied Mattie and a slight flush crept up her neck as she recalled the ardour of the night before. It did not escape Queenie's sharp eyes, "And what about Bill?" she asked with a knowing grin. For a moment Matilda looked sad as she remembered the devastation of Bill's realisation that she knew exactly what he had been doing. They had not spoken about it directly but each had affirmed their love and commitment to the other and they had reached a tacit agreement that his indiscretion would not come between them. Their marriage was of paramount importance to them both and the newly commissioned task of preparing sermons for the Archbishop had the effect of drawing them closer and would allow the necessary healing to happen. It would take time for Matilda to trust Bill again but he was determined to not do anything at all to give her cause to doubt him. "He's coping," replied Mattie. "We'll be okay," she said.

Queenie hugged her friend again saying, "Come on my dear, these pastries are not going to bake themselves!"

~

Over in Partington Hall, borrowed chairs and trestle tables were being delivered to the ballroom in readiness for the advent of the caterers who would arrive early the following morning. Dusty and dishevelled, Amy and Imogen discussed how best to arrange the furniture and where to place the serving tables while Grace sat in her wheelchair and directed proceedings from the doorway. "Not there silly!" she barked, "That's where I'm going to display the photographs and other memorabilia. Did you remember to bring some bits and pieces from Hingemont House?"

"Of course," replied Imogen, "they're in that box on the table over there. I hope they're the sort of thing you wanted? I put in a few of her prized ornaments, some of her WI badges and a few of the less personal letters that she wrote to Granddad during the war. There were dozens to choose from!"

"Humph!" was the only response from Grace but she looked moderately pleased with Imogen's contribution. Anyone would have thought that it was her responsibility to organise the memorial, but perhaps in a way it was. After all she had known Ada much longer than either Imogen or Max and despite her former misgivings; she was secretly pleased to be involved in providing her long-standing friend with a splendid occasion and grand farewell.

When all was prepared, Imogen hurried home to be sure that she was available to greet her guests as they arrived.

The first to appear were Catherine and Mum, who was looking both exhausted and confused. She didn't seem to know where she was or why she was there and it took all three of them, Imogen, Max and Caroline, to settle her into Gran's bedroom where it had been decided she would be best accommodated. Once she was ensconced, Max stayed with her while the two women organised her belongings and checked the exhaustive list of instructions and medication the nursing home had provided for her care regime.

Just as Max reappeared to tell them that Mum had fallen asleep, the doorbell rang again and there were Archie, Avril and the two children. Carly bounced up and down excitedly, hugging first Imogen and then her aunty Caroline whilst asking where she would sleep and could she see GG and why was Granny in bed when it was only seven o'clock? Stoic Simon sucked his thumb and gazed hungrily at the cling-film covered sandwiches that awaited further arrivals.

A short time later, after the entrance of Cousin Molly, the house was bustling with the business of guests and the gentle hum of conversation between people who had not met each other for some time. There were animated anecdotes to be recounted, exciting or sad stories to be told and a lot of catching up and filling in of events and happenings in the time between the last meeting and this.

At one point there was a lull in the discussions and after a pause, Imogen said quietly, "Wouldn't Gran have loved this? Us all being here together again." There was a momentary silence before Avril swept Simon up into her arms and said, "Come along Carly; bedtime."

The service was arranged for Twelve noon the following day and so it was generally agreed that an early night was in order. Imogen showed each of the guests to their rooms before climbing the little spiral staircase to her own room at the top of the turret. She could have removed herself to one of the first floor guest rooms but she felt comfortable up here and appreciated a sense of isolation from the hubbub of families below her. She hoped Mum would sleep through the night and perhaps tomorrow she would have a better idea of where she was and why.

Slipping between the sheets, she patted the bed to invite Benjy to join her. She needed the comfort of his warm body nestled behind her knees and he was as obviously unsettled as was she by the surprising number of people who were now occupying his spaces. Despite her determination to provide for Gran a wonderful celebration of her life and for everyone to show their appreciation of what that extraordinary woman had achieved, she would be rather pleased when it was all over and done with.

~

Not far away, in her cosy bedroom in Partington Hall, Amy was surprised to hear the ringtone of her mobile phone and even more surprised to hear Arthur's voice. "I just wanted to make sure you're okay," he said, "you seemed a bit upset at work this morning." She was about to respond that it was rather late to be calling her when she realised that it was actually only nine thirty and so not really late at all. "I'm fine, thanks," she replied. "It's kind of you to be concerned but really I'm quite alright. I was just a little preoccupied with all the funeral arrangements and Mum can be a bit demanding at times. Do you know when she will get her mobility scooter back? She's rather inconvenienced without it."

This wasn't really the sort of conversation Arthur had hoped for but he told himself he should have realised that Amy has no idea how he is feeling about her. How could she possibly know? He hadn't said or done anything to indicate that theirs was anything more than a working relationship other than that their respective parents' were best of friends.

"I think she should have it back in time for the service tomorrow," he said, "I asked Peterson to be sure she wouldn't be put out for too long and reminded him that tomorrow is an important day. He assured me he'd do his best for her."

176

"Thank you," said Amy, "I'll see you tomorrow then. Bye for now; good night." She ended the call and lay back on her pillows, 'That was strange,' she thought and then suddenly she was sitting bolt upright, "Oh!" she exclaimed out loud and then began to giggle. It wasn't really such a ludicrous idea, was it? He is a lot older than her but he is quite good looking and, well, maybe... She fell asleep with a small smile on her face while poor Arthur hardly slept at all having decided that it had been a stupid idea to phone her and he'd probably completely jeopardised any possibility of anything at all.

Chapter 31

In Memoriam

The service had been beautiful with inspired music choices and emotional words from Bill Banner and an impressive eulogy from Max. Contributions from various members of the village community who had had links with Gran; through the church, the WI, Scouting and many other social aspects of village life, made clear the fulfilling and varied life that Ada had led. Her interests were wide and she had been successful in many different walks of life. There were humorous anecdotes as well as other stories that demonstrated her compassion for all things both living and inanimate. There had been no specific mention of the nature of her demise, for which Imogen in particular was grateful, and no one asked for details. There were many expressions of regret at her passing and without exception everyone agreed that she would be greatly missed.

The reception held in the beautiful ballroom at Partington Hall, was magnificent. The setting was absolutely appropriate, the floral arrangements stunning and the food delicious. Imogen could not have been better pleased and particularly so since it had all been organised for her. She could never thank Grace and Amy enough. Above all, she knew that Gran would have been delighted with it all.

Even the clearing away had been taken care of and the ballroom returned to its former, rather bare, status soon after the final guests had departed.

The whirring of Grace's scooter, which had been duly returned to her early that morning, preceded her entrance and gave Imogen time to wipe away the tears that betrayed her emotions and gather the remaining flowers into her arms to disguise her distress. It didn't work!

"No need to cry my girl," intoned the venerable old lady, "it's upsetting for us all. So very final. She's gone and that's it." She sniffed and dabbed a lacy handkerchief across her own face before continuing, "All that remains now is for us to find out how it happened. However, there's something I think you should know before you leave today; before you attend the inquest next week. I don't want you to have another shock. You've had enough of those already! Come into the parlour, it's more comfortable in there and Amy has made some tea. Too much wine makes us all muddle headed – we need to dilute it a bit."

Imogen followed Grace across the hall and into the parlour; a cosy room with a bright fire burning in the hearth. She sat in the indicated chair as Grace manoeuvred her scooter next to the opposite one before heaving herself from one seat to the other. Once she was settled she began, "One day, not long before that awful Friday, your gran came to me and said she had something to tell me. I could see that she was upset and it wasn't like her so I stopped what I was doing, something pretty unimportant I expect, and invited her to take tea and talk. It's funny how tea always seems to placate and soothe as well as loosening the tongue." Imogen nodded and smiled a watery smile as she took the proffered cup from Amy who then sat down on the edge of a small sofa.

"Go on," she invited.

"Ada told me that she'd been to the doctor a few days earlier. She said that she had a problem and that she wasn't sure it could be fixed. She didn't go into any details despite my probing. She was rather a private person when it came to health or body matters but it was clear that she was more worried than she was letting on. Anyway, that's really all I can tell you. I don't know what it might mean or whether it could have had anything to do with how she died. Probably not, but I thought you should know in case anything comes to light at the inquest. They can be pretty upsetting occasions you know. I had to attend one for my dear husband although that was a very long time ago now and anyway, we knew what he had died from." Grace sniffed again but Amy looked across to Imogen and raised her eyes as if to say, 'there wasn't much love lost between my parents!'

Imogen smiled weakly at Amy and thanked Grace for being so thoughtful before excusing herself saying, "I must get back to my houseguests. They'll be wondering where I am. I can't thank you enough for all you've done for Gran and for me and

I'll pop round to see you again very soon if that's alright with you?"

"I'll be pleased to see you anytime," replied Grace, "you're like your grandmother, you know."

~

The evening passed without any serious event. There was more chit chat and reminiscing about school holidays spent with Gran and Granddad; the turret room they shared, the feather bed, the ghost stories and the adventures roaming the open farm land that surrounded the village of Hingemont. One by one the cousins drifted away and home and Mum, who had been dozing in a comfortable chair near the fireplace suddenly sat up and said, "Right then. I like your company but I don't like your hours! I'm going upstairs to say goodnight to my mother and then I'm off to bed." The brief moment of lucidity surprised the assembled company and for a minute or two no one rose to help her or to remind her that her mother was no longer there. However, as she made her way unsteadily across the lounge, Max took her elbow and guided her out of the room.

"What will you do?" asked Molly, "I don't suppose Aunty Mimi will ever recover her memory, will she?"

"I'm afraid not," replied Imogen, "but until I know what's to happen to the house here and have made my own plans for the future, I think she'll have to return to Sundown. They do take good care of her there but I can see how much more confused she has become. I think she would benefit from seeing us more regularly; I'm sure we remind her of how things used to be. It's so sad really since she's very young to suffer Alzheimer's."

"Are you thinking of staying up here then?" enquired Archie. The subject hadn't been broached before but now that the question had been asked, Imogen realised that that was exactly what she had been thinking. "Maybe," she said, "but it's dependent on a lot of things, so time will tell."

The conversation turned to more mundane matters, such as what time various parties would be leaving the following day and how could they best thank Mattie and Queenie for their splendid help with feeding them all during their stay. It was agreed that Caroline would order some flowers for them both, to be delivered to their respective homes early the next week. Imogen would find out Queenie's address on the pretext of wanting to write a thank you note or perhaps of wanting to add Queenie and Eric to her Christmas card list. Christmas would arrive all too soon and Imogen would be keen to acknowledge her new Hingemont friends when the time and opportunity arose.

It was only a short time later when the assembled company had retired for the night and once more Imogen found herself alone with her thoughts. As she lay back on the soft downy pillows, she allowed the tears to fall unheeded. If only Gran were still here, there were so many things she would like to ask her about.

Chapter 32

Johnsborough County Court

The day dawned crisp and bright. It was cold and Amy's breath puffed out before her as though she were a small dragon. She blew on her hands and stamped her feet whilst she waited for Arthur and the rest of the party to arrive. She smiled to herself as she thought of Arthur and his advances toward her which had become increasingly attentive, amorous and almost ardent. There had been a flower on her desk, chocolates in the small office kitchen and offers of coffee when usually she would have made some for him. He was clumsy in his wooing but she appreciated his attempts and was not averse to letting him continue for a while. She knew that she would eventually accept his invitation to dinner and that there was probably a relationship in the offing but she was not in any hurry to precipitate a change of circumstances; for the time being, she was happy with the way things were.

Then there they were. All five of them arrived in one vehicle having been warned that parking was at a premium in the small Court car park. Accordingly they had arranged to meet at Arthur's office and travelled together from Manton to Johnsborough.

Imogen looked very smart in her long black coat and Max and Archie were wearing business suits. Molly was a little less formally attired but nevertheless looked neat and appropriate. The small group were led by Arthur, up the courthouse steps and into a waiting area. There were formalities to attend to and security to process before they were eventually led into the courtroom where Inspector Peterson, Helen Carter and the coroner awaited their entrance. Shortly afterwards, Charlie, accompanied by Bill Banner and Otto Vasovich with Igor to translate where necessary were ushered into the room.

Although it was ostensibly a formal occasion, the atmosphere was friendly and far less intimidating than Imogen had feared it might have been. The proceedings began with the Coroner stating the case number and Gran's full name; Ada Imogen Springfield. With a start, Imogen realised she hadn't before heard Gran's middle name and suddenly understood why Gran had always appeared to have a special connection with her eldest granddaughter.

Having outlined his findings and the details of his post mortem; the only questionable point being the presence of traces of CBT in Ada's blood which was dismissed on the grounds of there not being sufficient quantities to have affected the outcome of an obvious death by a significant blow to the head, the coroner then called upon Inspector Peterson to give a brief report on his investigations into the possible cause of the blow that had ultimately killed her.

Charlie was called upon to explain the bloodstains on his clothes and shovel and with prompting from Bill it was made quite clear that the stains were from a dead badger and nothing to do with Ada at all. Peterson produced forensic evidence to substantiate the findings including a report of the same blood being found on the bumper of Grace Murdock's mobility scooter and her eventual confession of having hit a badger earlier the same day. This was followed by a series of questions to Otto, who through Igor, was able to explain that the fallen ladder had been repositioned against the church wall, thus disguising the fact that it had almost certainly played a part in Ada's demise.

Finally Peterson produced further forensic evidence that the blood stain found on a nearby rock was indeed that of Ada Springfield and therefore a blow from the offending boulder was likely to have been the ultimate cause of her death.

After a few minutes silence in which everyone in the room appeared to hold their breath, the coroner spoke. "I think it is pretty clear from the evidence you have provided and the witness statements heard here today, that we are looking at a case of accidental death. I surmise that Mrs Springfield, was walking around the church in search of a missing key and because she was looking down into the long grass rather than where she was going, she bumped into the aforementioned ladder which then fell across her path, knocking her from her feet as it did so, and thus causing her to fall and hit her head on an unfortunately positioned stone as she did so. We can't be absolutely sure since there were no immediate witnesses to the event but I have no reason to suspect foul play and it is my intention therefore to record a misadventure which resulted in a large contusion to Mrs Springfield's head and subsequently, her accidental death."

There was a combined sigh of relief from those present. Despite their general opinion that the outcome was a foregone conclusion, there had always been the possibility of some previously undisclosed information that could have muddied the waters and caused further complications. It was altogether a much appreciated and satisfactory result and there was a lightness in the steps of all those who left the courtroom a mere thirty minutes after first entering.

~

All that remained was for Imogen to decide her future which would be determined in part by the contents of Gran's will. And so it was that she, Max, Archie, Cousin Molly and Arthur returned to the offices of Barnes and Son, in Manton, and were met there shortly afterwards by Amy who quickly provided coffee and biscuits for all.

Arthur was rather enjoying his position of authority. It didn't come naturally to him to be assertive and dictatorial, although he was adept at acting out his role as lawyer in the courtroom. In the office it was quite another matter and his naturally deprecating manner usually came to the fore. However, on this occasion he knew the news that he was going to impart to the assembled company and he knew that there would be some pleasant surprises as well as some minor disappointment.

The first surprise was his, when Amy pulled up a chair next to his own on the side of his desk facing the family. She placed it a little closer than was strictly necessary and he could smell the soft perfume of her hair as she leant across to pull the folder of papers closer to his reach. She smiled at him and he smiled back before he opened the folder and began to read.

"I, Ada Imogen Springfield, being of sound mind, on this twentieth day of March 2012, do declare that this is my last will and testament and succeeds all and any other prior documents.

I leave my house, Hingemont House, to my grandchildren collectively, however, should she so choose, my granddaughter, Imogen Emma Walker, has the right to continue to live in the property until such time as she no longer chooses to do so." Imogen gasped! How could Gran have possibly known that she would be living in Hingemont House at the time the Will would be read?

Arthur continued to read, "During her residence at Hingemont House, she will pay a stipend of one quarter of her income divided between any and all surviving Springfield cousins." It was typical of Ada to ensure that Imogen must pay her way in terms of rent and she smiled wryly to herself. Molly and her brothers remained silent and expressionless.

"The vast collection of ornaments and other bric-a-brac, catalogued and stored in my late husband's study are to be divided amongst those relatives who may wish to take some memorabilia. The remaining items should be sold and the revenue shared between grandchildren, with the exception of Imogen who is to have the Faberge egg that is in my bedroom." On hearing this, Max and Archie visibly relaxed as both were in no doubt as to the value of some of the items tucked away in Granddad's snug. There would be plenty there to provide a tidy sum for each of them and their cousins.

"Finally," Arthur read on, "I have some significant investments, the details of which are in the hands of Barnes and Son." Here he looked up and nodded at the listeners before, "These are to be sold as necessary to provide donations to Hingemont Parish Church and the village hall, Hingemont Primary School, the WI and the Scouting movement. I would also like to make available in perpetuity, a small music scholarship bursary at Wendle School. Should there be any remaining funds after these expenses, they should be reinvested and any income used to maintain Hingemont House and keep it in good order until such time as it is sold."

"There are a few other minor bequests, such as a small sum for Charlie, but the rest of the details needn't concern us here today," said Arthur as he closed the folder and rested back in his chair. No one spoke for several minutes until Archie leant forward saying, "Looks like you've got it made old girl," as he patted Imogen's knee. She suddenly found she was crying again and Molly flung her arms around her cousin and hugged her tight. "Gran was an amazing lady. She knew us all so well and you, of all of us, deserve to live in that house! I don't begrudge you a single part of it and I know the others will agree with me. You've had a pretty rough time recently but I've seen how happy you are here and how the villagers seem to have accepted you into their ranks already. Perhaps you should arrange for Aunty Mimi to come and live with you too?"

At that suggestion Imogen looked horrified and suddenly everyone was talking at once and all were agreeing that Gran had been wise and generous in her sharing of her assets. Unanimously they said that Mimi should be in a nursing home as she needed far more care than it was reasonable to expect any one of them to provide. There were laughter and tears, speculation and disbelief as Arthur indicated the amount invested and the possible value of the collectables. All in all, everyone agreed that they could not have had a more satisfactory conclusion to a very unfortunate state of affairs. Poor Gran, but how wonderfully thoughtful and careful she had been at her end; just as she had always been.

Chapter 33

Secret of the Snail

Hingemont House seemed very quiet and empty when all the guests were departed. Even Max had gone home with his wife and mother although he had promised to return as soon as he could to help with distributing the collectables. They would all need to be photographed so that the cousins could choose which they would like to keep, if any. However, right then, Imogen found herself wandering through the rooms and wondering how she might rearrange things to suit her own style. She would need to find a job nearby but her copywriting could be done online and that would provide her with a small income in the meantime. She was beginning to realise just how fortunate she had been to be provided with this wonderful house for as long as she chose to stay but at times she was also aware of just how large and isolated the building could be.

Suddenly she was overpoweringly lonely, so calling Benjy and pulling on her warm overcoat and boots, cramming a woolly hat on her head and a scarf around her neck, she set off for a walk. Much as on that first morning; how long ago it seemed now but in reality it had only been a few weeks, she paid little attention to the direction in which her feet were taking her.

Deep in thought, head bent against the cold wind and marching briskly to keep out the chill, she found herself entering the Churchyard. There she was surprised to see Charlie tending the headstones and clipping the long grass from along the edges of the paths. He greeted her shyly but suddenly let out a great bellow that caused her to jump out of her skin. "Gerroff you little scamp!" he yelled and gesticulated wildly at something just out of Imogen's sight. "Bloody little blighter," he muttered and turning bright red, "beggin' yer pardon, Miss," as he realised his inappropriate use of language.

Imogen smiled and asked who he was shouting at.

"It's that Sammy child," Charlie replied thickly, "always messin' about in the Churchyard and up to no good I've no doubt."

"Leave him to me," offered Imogen, "I'll see if I can find him and see what he's playing at. It's probably just some private little adventure, I'm sure there's not much harm he can do in here." Charlie muttered some incomprehensible reply but he seemed happy enough to let Imogen deal with the recalcitrant boy.

A short while later, she found Sammy bent over a mound in the corner of the Churchyard. He was hammering a roughly made cross into the ground at the head of the mound. A placard attached to the cross with a large amount of sticky tape bore the misspelt and uneven legend, 'Here Lys Brok ver Bagger'.

He scrambled to his feet and wiped his muddy hands down his trousers as Imogen quietly asked him, "What are you doing?"

"Can't yer see lady?" he retorted, "I'm markin' 'is grave. All graves should 'ave crosses on 'em. 'Overwise no one won't know who they were."

"Of course," agreed Imogen and made a mental note to chase up the stonemason who was supposed to be making a memorial stone for Gran. There would be no grave since her remains had been cremated but they had agreed to plant a tree on the village green and a memorial would be placed beneath it.

Sammy brought her out of her reverie by tugging on her arm, "Do yer wanna see somefink?" he asked, "I know a secret and I'll tell yer if'n you want."

Wondering what sort of a secret Sammy might be about to reveal she followed him back into the main Graveyard and across to the dry stone wall that surrounded the Churchyard plot. As they reached the point furthest from the Church, he knelt down and pulled some long grass away from the near the base of the wall. He carefully removed a fairly large stone which he placed on the ground before reaching into the cavity he had revealed. Dry grass and some bird seed fell to the ground before his hand reappeared clutching... the snail; the snail with a secret hiding place, in a secret hiding place; but why?

Imogen gasped, "Why?" as Sammy carefully stroked the solid back of the inanimate object and, "When..." she stammered, "What... but..." she didn't seem able to string a sentence together and Sammy just stared at her as he continued to stroke the snail.

"I was worried about 'im," he whispered, "it were raining and 'e was out in the cold. I made 'im an 'ouse there in the wall so's I knew 'e'd be warm and dry." He looked imploringly at Imogen, half expecting the remonstration he was so very and unhappily used to. But no admonishment came. Instead Imogen knelt beside him and very gently took the snail from his hands. "May I look?" she asked and without waiting for an answer she pressed the button under the snail's chin which released a catch and opened the chamber inside the snail's rounded shell. Sammy peered over her shoulder and gasped as she revealed not only the Church door key but a folded piece of paper.

"Did you put that in there?" she asked Sammy but, "No!" he replied, round eyed and surprised, "I didn' know it could open!" he said.

Quite suddenly Sammy was no longer interested as Benjy, having finished his own canine investigation, bounded up to the boy and began to lick his face. Sammy was captivated. Here was a real live animal he could play with. Much better than the toys and ornaments he was usually obliged to pretend needed his care. He would be a vet one day – no matter what that 'orrible Miss Lester said...

"Well I never!" said Mattie as Imogen told her the tale of the snail and its hiding place, "To think how things might have turned out if it hadn't disappeared in the first place!" For a moment the two were silent as they both realised the implication of Mattie's words; Gran might still be, Imogen might not be, (Bill might not have... no that was silly, he probably already had...) everything would have been completely different – well almost everything.

"It's funny how things happen as they must," Imogen mused and then unfolded the small piece of paper that had been inside the snail. The snail that now stood on Mattie's kitchen table together with the missing key.

"This was inside the snail too," she said as she handed the note to Matilda.

Mattie read aloud:

"To whoever finds this first; perhaps you will keep my secret to yourself until such time as everyone has found out. I don't want any fuss and I don't want to distress or inconvenience anyone so I'm choosing this unusual way of letting each of you know that my days on this earth are numbered.

I have recently been diagnosed with a brain cancer. Unfortunately mine is the inoperable, aggressive variety and I will become increasingly unstable and clumsy over the next few months. You will notice a change in me but please don't alter the

*way you treat me. I've had a good life and I'm
ready to go to wherever the next place is.*

*Don't feel sorry for me – I'm fine, I really
am. I'll say farewell to you now since all too soon I
may not be able to. Thank you for all that we have
shared over the years.*

Goodbye my friend.

Ada xxx

*PS please put this note back where you found
it so that each of you may find it in turn. Don't
discuss me; just love me!"*

"Oh my goodness!" Mattie could hardly
believe what she had just read. Tears streamed
down her face and she blindly passed a tissue to
Imogen who was similarly affected.

"Wasn't she amazing?" asked Imogen as
soon as she had recovered a little of her composure,
"And don't you see? It explains something that I've
been puzzling over. At the inquest the coroner said
Gran had traces of CBT in her system. It was rather
glossed over since it didn't directly contribute to the
accident, but now I suppose that it would have been
to control the pain from her cancer. It all makes a
lot more sense now. Impossibly sad – but I think I
understand and I think I'm glad I didn't know too. I
couldn't have borne to see her suffer and gradually
decline. This way she retained her dignity right to
the end – even if that end was not quite what she
anticipated."

Chapter 34

Hingemont – fifteen years later

Layla Lester pushed the empty coffee mug away from her and pulled the pile of books closer. For how many years now had she been marking books on a Sunday afternoon? Far too many it seemed; especially when the sun was shining and she would much rather be working in her small garden. At that thought, she made a decision. The books could wait, it was too nice an afternoon to be stuck indoors; she would enjoy the fresh air and mark the books tonight.

The warmth of the sun fell on her upturned face as she went out into her small front garden. Secateurs in hand, she would prune the roses which grew in abundance and scented the air with their fragrance. She smiled as she heard the chatter of young voices of the children playing outside and the rhythmic squeak and groan of a trampoline in someone's garden. Lawn mowers hummed and Charlie's spade clattered on stones in the Churchyard. Charlie had become slower and slower these days and he appeared to be working in the Churchyard all day every day. Nevertheless, he still kept it neat and tidy and he took especial care of the tree and commemorative stone bearing the legend; "Ada Imogen Springfield, 1924 – 2018, Beloved wife, mother and Gran."

Layla could hear horse's hooves approaching and Helen Carter waved at her as she took Guinness, now a very elderly horse, for his once a week ride through the village. Some years ago, Guinness had been replaced by a very smart little electric car that provided Helen, now rather broader in the beam than was fair to the old horse, with quicker and more efficient transport to and from the various incidents to which she was called.

Emily, the new vicar's wife, could be seen approaching from the Manse, and from the basket she carried wafted a tantalising smell of baking. "What a beautiful afternoon," she called as soon as she was within earshot, "I've brought you some scones since I've baked far too many and Frank will start getting fat if I feed him anymore!" Her bright laugh rang out and Layla chuckled with her as she took the proffered basket and invited Emily to join her for a cup of tea.

"Oh no thank you," she replied, "I need to get back and have the children ready for Evensong. Are you coming tonight?"

"No, not this time," Layla was uncomfortably aware that Bill and Matilda Banner would be visiting on this occasion since they had been staying with Queenie and Eric for a few days. Despite that it was almost fourteen years since they had been relocated to a diocese some fifty miles away, Layla still felt ashamed when she remembered how nearly she had destroyed their marriage. She would stay away and allow the other villagers to reminisce and enjoy an evening talking about the good old days. 'And they were good times,' she thought to herself, 'but these times are better.' There is comfortability in growing older, a lessening of the need to make a good impression, to be attractive. There is a confidence that comes with maturity and the knowledge that everyone makes mistakes and it is more important to learn from those errors than to regret that you made them. She would not have chosen to live alone for all these years, but she had forged friendships with the villagers, was respected, accepted and was entrusted with their children's education. Pamela Postlethwaite had been an absolutely wonderful source of advice and guidance, once Layla had understood that she must accept the ways and traditions of a village such as Hingemont. Even after her retirement (eight years ago already) Pamela had continued to visit the school regularly and help out whenever there was a need. Claire Watts, the new infant teacher, did her best but Layla could see her struggling with the same sorts of issues that she herself had battled with as a newcomer all those years ago. She determined to help Claire as she herself had been helped.

Later that evening, Layla returned to the pile of books and lifted the first from the pile. 'Miriam Marchant' she read and thought to herself, 'Ah, Mimi, Imogen's daughter. What a bright little child she is!'

Imogen and her husband, Christopher, had been married in Hingemont Church ten years ago and still resided in Hingemont House. Little Mimi, named for her grandmother, was now eight years old and her five year old brother, Kit, had just this summer term, begun in the reception class at Hingemont School. Although many things had changed over the years, the continuity of families residing in the village never ceased to amaze Layla. The Jenkins family still lived in the cottages at the far end of the village even though Sammy and the other children that Layla had first met were all grown up and flown the nest. Enough of them remained tied to Hingemont to provide continuity and that connection was valued by those who appreciated such things.

~

Over in Partington Hall, on the edge of the next village, Amy and Arthur sat down to an evening in front of the blazing log fire. They hadn't been blessed with children of their own but the ballroom had been converted into a pre-school nursery and playgroup. Arthur continued to work at Barnes and Son in Manton but a new and efficient secretary had been employed full time to take Amy's place. Amy leant back in her comfortable chair and sighed.

"Problems?" enquired Arthur.

"No, not really," Amy replied, "it's just that I miss seeing Imogen when she brings Tommy."

"Why do you miss her?" Arthur, in typical fashion, had not taken in the implication in his wife's words.

"Tommy is attending school now, silly!" Amy teased good-naturedly, "but never mind. Things have to change, it's only natural." She reached over the side of her chair to fondle the head of Pippa, the little terrier that looked so much like her beloved Pip who had died soon after Grace had passed away. Was it really four years ago already?

"I'm going to visit Mary tomorrow after work," she changed the subject, "do you want to come with me? I'm sure she'd be pleased to see you. It's deadly dull in that nursing home. I'm not sure how Mimi put up with it for so long; but then I suppose she didn't really know where she was so maybe it didn't affect her in the same way."

There was no response from Arthur except for a gentle snore as the newspaper slipped from his lap onto the floor. Amy smiled to herself and picked up the novel she was reading. It was going to be another quiet evening.

~

There was a sudden screech of brakes and a loud bang right outside Layla's front door. School books were scattered across the room and a glass of wine toppled over as she leapt to her feet to see what had caused the interruption.

A young man scrambled out from the misshapen wreckage of a car and she was met by half of her garden wall piled up immediately outside her front door. 'So much for the carefully tended roses' flashed through her mind.

"Oh my goodness! Are you hurt?" She expressed her concern for the youth. Blood dripped down from a gash in his forehead but he shook his head saying, "I'm ok. The car isn't. Dad will be furious. But where is the cat?"

"Cat?" and "Oh!" as realisation hit her. "Willow, where are you? Come to mummy my baby." Layla had acquired Willow when the school's cat had produced kittens. To be more precise, Willow had adopted Layla and was regularly to be found curled up on Layla's office chair or asleep in her bag of books, making it quite clear that Layla was her human and that they belonged together.

However, Willow was a hunter and was often seen chasing mice or voles along the hedges. She was adept at catching the small rodents but had absolutely no road sense whatsoever. Several times Layla had been alarmed by a screech of brakes or a fisted horn as a vehicle narrowly avoided hitting the little cat. This time it seemed the driver hadn't been quite so lucky or so careful. Perhaps he had just been driving too fast but at this precise point Layla couldn't care less about the reasoning; her only concern was for Willow.

Having made quite sure that the driver didn't need urgent medical attention and that he was busily telephoning his father to get some help with the car and his predicament, Layla began to hunt for her cat.

Chapter 35

Retribution

Layla sat in the bland waiting room and once again checked the small bundle wrapped in a soft towel and held firmly to her breast. Yes, she was still breathing. Why is it that all too often we don't fully appreciate what we have until it is on the verge of being taken from us? Suddenly, Layla realised how Matilda must have felt all those years ago and another pang of guilt flushed her cheeks. She bent her head low over the tiny form cradled in her arms and wept.

"Mrs Lester?" A tall white coated man spoke softly and held open the door to his surgery, "Come through," he invited and she rose unsteadily and made her way into the room. Smells of disinfectant, not unpleasant, assailed her nose as she placed the towel wrapped figure on the inspection bench.

"What happened here?" asked the vet and Layla lifted her head to begin to explain.

He was very tall and to begin with her eyes only reached the end of the stethoscope draped around his neck. Gradually, and blinking through the tears, she lifted her gaze, past the name badge pinned to his overall and up to his face. She didn't recognise him at first; older and bearded, he was nothing like the small boy she had known but the name badge confirmed what she realised with a start. Sammy Jenkins!

He smiled at her as he carefully examined the injured kitten, "Don't worry," he said, "she'll be fine. We all will be..."

Printed in Great Britain
by Amazon

23391270R00112